"It's our very own paradise island!"

Then, daring to tease, Laraine added, "We're a long way from the schoolroom now."

"True," Neal said, grinning.

He was very close, and looking deep into her eyes, he became suddenly serious. His lips came down on hers gently, tenderly, but in a way that left her vaguely unsatisfied, so that when he finally drew away she asked breathlessly, "What was that for?"

"You didn't deserve the manhandling I gave you the other day," he murmured huskily. "You're a sweet kid, and I'm sorry."

Whether by accident or design he was still very close. After a long, lingering moment he said gruffly, "Apologies over. Am I forgiven?"

"Yes, Neal," Laraine replied, wildly happy. His next words, however, quickly shattered the near realization of her dreams. . . .

ROUMELIA LANE
is also the author of these
Harlequin Romances

1180—ROSE OF THE DESERT
1212—HIDEAWAY HEART
1262—HOUSE OF THE WINDS
1290—A SUMMER TO LOVE
1338—SEA OF ZANJ
1395—TERMINUS TEHRAN
1479—THE SCENTED HILLS
1547—CAFE MIMOSA
1654—IN THE SHADE OF THE PALMS
1745—NURSE AT NOONGWALLA
1823—ACROSS THE LAGOON
1920—HARBOUR OF DECEIT
1984—THE TENANT OF SAN MATEO
2107—BAMBOO WEDDING

and this
Harlequin Presents

91—STORMY ENCOUNTER

Dream Island

by

ROUMELIA LANE

Harlequin Books

TORONTO • LONDON • LOS ANGELES • AMSTERDAM
SYDNEY • HAMBURG • PARIS • STOCKHOLM • ATHENS • TOKYO

Original hardcover edition published in 1981
by Mills & Boon Limited

ISBN 0-373-02460-6

Harlequin edition published February 1982

Printed in U.S.A.

CHAPTER ONE

THE ocean stretched away, its range of blues and greens infinite and unbelievable. It was a seascape that no dappled countryside could rival for loveliness, though the views of palm and pine-clad shores dotted with white colonial-style houses were dazzling in themselves.

Laraine dug her bare feet into the pink sand and watched it shower away from her toes disconsolately. She had thought it would be better here so far away from England, but it wasn't. She couldn't stop thinking about Richard. The thought that she would never see him again or hear his breezy voice brought a glisten of tears to her eyes that no tropical paradise could dispel.

If anything the views around her made her feel worse. They were a reminder that the world could be beautiful and that one could be so dreadfully alone in it. Of course she had Adele. Her small face looked glummer still. It was awful to think that she had no love for her sister-in-law. How could she have when but for Adele her brother would still be alive?

Laraine had never wanted Richard to take up motor racing. Young as she was, she knew that he hadn't the temperament for it. But he had wanted to impress Adele, and because she had grown tired of him as a husband she had gladly nurtured his passion for speed-racing, supplying him with all the money he needed from her vast fortune just to have him out of the way.

It had been different when they had first met. Tall and handsome, with fair good looks, Richard had been the perfect foil for Adele's dark beauty. Despite the fact that he was several years younger than her she was soon wearing him on her arm at the society outings as she might flaunt one of her prized pieces of jewellery. Richard had fallen wildly in love with her, and when there was something he wanted he could be very persuasive. He must have managed to communicate some of his desperation to her, for she had consented to marry him in a matter of weeks. But Adele was the type of woman who quickly grew bored with anything that became permanent in her life, and it wasn't long before she was pursuing other romantic attachments, and by this time Richard had been bitten by the speed bug.

Her face white at the memory, Laraine recalled that fateful afternoon on the misty race track. Adele had taken it well. It had been her idea to leave the November drizzle of London behind and depart for some part of the world that would prove more amusing. Laraine had shrunk from the thought of visiting some millionaire playground; she wanted to stay near all the things that Richard had loved. But Adele had been adamant. 'Look, child, it won't do you any good moping around the old haunts,' she had said pettishly. 'Besides, I can't very well go alone. You know I don't like to drive. And there'll be a dozen and one things I'll be too busy to attend to myself.'

Laraine knew all too well what these words were meant to imply. The 'dozen and one things' would include organising Adele's wardrobe, planning her meals, typing out her diet sheets, arranging hairdressing appointments. . . . Since her brother had married Adele, Laraine had become more or less her unpaid maid. She hadn't minded while she had been with Richard, sharing the smell of engines with him in the oil pits, watching his face as he viewed the other speed machines. But now. . . .

She jumped up quickly and began to scuff around in the sand. Thinking about it didn't help; she should know that by now. She was ready to accept that it was better to get away from everything that reminded her of her brother, but they had been here in the Bahamas a week and she was no nearer coming to terms with the appalling gap in her life than she had been at the start. Yet it wouldn't be so bad if she could know that Adele felt some small grief.

She blinked the damp from her lashes, then turned back towards the house. She at least missed Richard—desperately so.

A small wicker gate closed off the rear entrance of an adjoining property and Laraine would not have given it a second glance but for the sight of something which caused her heart, already over-tender, to constrict. It must have been the ugliest little dog she had seen in her life, its coat being mottled in every shade of grey and brown and its ears too big for its small head. But its eyes were liquid with pleading as though it would draw attention to its prominent ribs and starved look.

That it was a stray trapped in the rambling property there was no doubt, for as she started to approach it, it took fright, and as though it was accustomed to being cuffed and kicked on its way, soon became lost in the tangle of long grass. But Laraine had noted its lolling tongue from heat and thirst, and she knew what it was like to be alone, so she rapidly scaled the gate with a view to coaxing it out into the open again.

In the few seconds it had taken her to put on her sandals there was no sign of the piebald scrap. Still she pushed her way on, sure that he couldn't be far away. She was in a field thick with tall flowering weeds of vivid yellow, and soon she saw that all was not lost, for the dog, though small, created considerable movement as he fled and his tracks were easy to spot through the waving weeds.

'Here, boy! Here, boy!' she crooned. 'Don't run away. I'm not going to hurt you.'

She followed cautiously so as not to give the impression of giving chase and after a while she was rewarded by a pause in the weeds' disturbance. She crouched and with the canopy of primrose above them, spotted him at last through the green stalks, a grey and brown splash with tail thumping half in eagerness and half in terror at her approach.

'That's right, you sit right there.' She talked to him encouragingly. 'You're too tired to run any more, I know, and really there's no need. You see, I want to be your friend . . . there! There's a good dog. . . . I told you it was all right. . . .'

She had barely drawn him to her to pat him reassuringly when the heavens exploded in some impending commotion which would have sent the dog scooting for safety again if she hadn't had the presence of mind to scoop him up in her arms.

Rising, she brought to a halt the obvious pursuers of the quivering scrap in her arms. Her glance clashed with the man in the lead, who was standing heaving breath into his overworked lungs. He was a muscular average height with an open-necked shirt showing a wedge of tanned chest. Behind him, rushing into view, came a couple of ebony-skinned house staff, one in kitchen attire brandishing a meat cleaver, the other a mean-looking garden rake.

The man in command made a gesture for them to hold back without moving his gaze. Laraine met it unflinchingly, hardly sparing a thought for what she must have looked like standing waist-high in yellow blossom, her old cotton beach top tied carelessly in a knot at her bare midriff, a frayed straw hat framing her unruly light brown hair, and the hounded recalcitrant clutched tightly in her arms.

The green eyes that met hers seemed to reflect the sea of green and yellow of the field but none of its summer softness. The man's comment, when it came, was directed at the dog, not at her. 'So we've finally run the little chiseller to earth!'

'No wonder his heart's going fit to burst,' Laraine retorted hotly, 'with you lot on his tail!'

'Put him down. He could give you a disease.' The stranger wasted no time on introductions.

'The only disease he's likely to have is man-made,' Laraine replied witheringly. 'Fear of the boot!'

'You're lucky he didn't bite you,' came the stern rejoinder.

'Well, he didn't,' Laraine said childishly. And because the plight of the quaking bundle in her arms was much akin to her own dejected frame of mind she flashed with tear-bright eyes, 'And I wouldn't have cared if he had!'

The man with the biting tones and grim countenance slackened his frame. He exhaled a loud sigh and remarked patiently, 'Look, youngster, I don't know what you're doing wandering around private property—*my* property—but I can tell you, you're going to do yourself no good holding on to that mangy street cur.'

'If you think I'm going to hand him over to you and your . . . cut-throats,' Laraine said dramatically, 'I'd . . . rather die first!'

The taciturn mouth twitched with something like humour, but in the next moment its owner was informing her harshly, 'It may interest you to know that the whelp you're protecting has just been found sneaking from the kitchen with the day's joint between his jaws.'

'There's a simple remedy for that,' Laraine said airily. 'Feed him.'

'If I were to provide board and lodgings for all the strays in Nassau you wouldn't be able to see the place for dogs.'

'What would that matter?' Irrationally Laraine let her glance roam around her, her sympathy confined to the one in her arms. 'With all this you can probably afford it.'

Another sigh escaped the lips of the property owner. With a gleam of tolerance he spoke to his hovering assistants. 'All right, boys, I'll attend to this. You can get back to the house.'

The white-clad servants exchanged comical glances with their boss, then retreated through the long grass. Laraine stood her ground with her small charge and when all was silent save for the murmur of the waves on the beach and the distant cry of sea birds she was told firmly, 'Put him down. I'm not going to hurt him.'

'No,' she said abruptly. 'He'll run away again. You know he will.'

'All right.' Placatingly the man searched his person and brought a tie from his pocket. 'How about this? It should hold him okay.'

'You'll have to make it so it doesn't choke him when he pulls,' said Laraine, relenting a little.

'Don't worry, I'll fix it.' Beside her he worked deftly, looping the tie round the dog's neck and securing it so that it would contain the nervous creature, but without discomfort. 'This is a knot I learned as a kid out with the fishing sloops.' His voice, close at hand, was deep-toned and not unpleasant.

At his male nearness Laraine was suddenly overcome with shyness. Arguing with the man at a distance had been one thing, but now the width of his shoulders blotted out the sun, and his muscular arms and brown hands worked with a capability that made her feel young and unsure of herself.

Fortunately her concern for the dog helped her to forget her awkwardness. 'Do you think he'll be able to walk?' she asked as they put him down, having second thoughts about his ability to run off. 'He's very weak.'

'He managed it this far,' her companion said drily. 'Having seen him sprint from the kitchen I'd say he's a lot tougher than you think.'

'But look at him!' She was full of compassion for the panting creature with his lolling tongue. 'He's gasping for water!'

'Well, we can remedy that.' With a nod the wide-shouldered individual indicated a point ahead. As though the dog knew there was something good in the offing he jerked forward and the three of them set off in single file through the tall grass.

After a fair stretch they came to a fenced-off area cultivated in a cluttered, haphazard way with blossoming fruit trees, vegetable patches, tumbling hibiscus bushes, potted shrubs and neat rows of flowers. They were at the rear of a rambling house and from what Laraine could see it had a mellowed and comfortable air as though it had belonged for many generations to one family.

There were signs of its antiquity in old stonework benches, wrought iron fitments and a well which proved to be the object of their trip. The owner lowered a bucket and brought up a sparkling shower which sent the dog into ecstatic whirls of delight. Over a chicken trough filled to the brim it lapped frantically for a while, then settled down to sip rhythmically, only lifting its head when it became aware that the masculine figure had moved off.

'If I remember rightly it was somewhere around this way that—yes, it's still here.' The man stooped beside a gap in the fence and retrieved the stolen joint which after taking a pen-knife from his pocket he proceeded to cut into strips.

'Here, let me.' As he worked on the stonework rim of the well, slicing off pieces of grass-smeared flesh, Laraine pointed out with adult perception, 'It will be bad for the poor little thing to eat too quickly in his starved condition. I'll give it to him slowly.'

'Watch what you're doing. He may be small, but he's got teeth.'

'He won't hurt me,' Laraine said confidently. 'He's too grateful for our help.'

The dog sniffed uncertainly at the cubes of meat in her hand as though he suspected it was a trick to prove that he was the culprit who had made off with it in the first place. Then, throwing all caution to the wind, he began to munch delicately, gulping and smacking his lips on each morsel.

'The trouble with dogs,' said the carver of the meat, 'is that they're adorable little perishers when they're puppies. Parents acquire them for their children, then when they grow up all angles and patchwork unsightliness like this young feller, they're shown the street and left to fend for themselves. There must be dozens of them roaming the island.'

'There would be two or three less if you allowed them to stay when they came looking,' Laraine suggested bluntly, 'instead of chasing them with a meat cleaver.'

'Maybe I would if I was here all the time. But I'm not.' Showing some irritation at having allowed himself to lapse into a mood of softness, his sharp reply pierced Laraine's sensitivity, and the tears which had never been far from the surface since she had involved herself in the plight of the dog rushed to her eyes. However, she continued to hold out scraps of meat as though oblivious to the foul mood of the man who had offered his assistance.

Propped against the well, he watched her, impatient at her trembling lip. He noted the boyish slimness of her young limbs, the trussed-up beach top and frayed shorts and the light dusting of gold on her skin. After a while he asked, 'What's your name?'

'Laraine,' she answered simply. The meat was fast disappearing. All her attention was with the dog.

'You can call me Neal,' he said laconically. He waited until the piebald scrap was wheezing with a full stomach. Laraine replaced what was left of the joint on the stonework rim of the well and said with girlish contentment, 'I bet he hasn't had such a good dinner in a long while.' She turned to go. 'I'm sorry if we've taken up your time. . . .'

'Not so fast!' Neal jerked from his lounging position. 'Now that you've attended to young hobo here there's something else that can't wait.' He disappeared towards a nearby doorway and returned a few seconds later with a towel and loofah and an ugly-looking bar of carbolic soap. 'Get your hands round that,' he tossed the latter to her and drew up water to assist with the sluicing. 'There's no telling what germs you may have subjected yourself to.'

Laraine did as he ordered lathering idly, but this apparently was not to Neal's satisfaction. 'Not just your fingertips,' he took the loofah, soaped it well and began to slap it around her bare midriff and along her arms, soapsuds and water flying everywhere.

'You don't have to be so bossy about it!' She snatched the loofah from him, tearful again. 'I know how to look after myself.'

'I doubt it,' he said grimly. 'You not only take a chance befriending a street cur who could have sunk his filthy teeth into you, you have to hug him to you as though he was the latest craze in furry toys.'

He rubbed her down vigorously with the towel as he might have done a younger brother, making no comment on her lack of fight to stand up to him, though her over-bright gaze, as she stood dried off and emanating a powerful smell of carbolic, caused him to eye her curiously.

She had been thinking about Adele and her abhorrence of anything on four legs. After some hesitation, during which she folded the towel neatly, she tried again, indicating the third member of the party who had been watching the abrupt exchanges with bright-eyed interest. 'I don't suppose you could find a home for him here?'

'No,' Neal said flatly. Something about her bowed head seemed to irritate him. 'It doesn't rest with me,' he tacked on shortly. 'It's up to the house staff to make those kind of decisions.'

Taking this as a roundabout refusal, Laraine straightened. 'Well, if you won't keep him, he'll have to go with me.' She looked beyond the house towards the road where the occasional car could be heard humming by and realising that this was unfamiliar territory to her she turned. 'I think I'll go back the way I came and make for the beach. I hope you don't mind if we borrow your tie?'

She had unfastened the makeshift lead from the stump it had been attached to and as the dog jerked forward, abounding with energy now Neal said, 'Here, let me.'

He took over, allowing the four-legged bundle of excitement full rein as they went out into the long grass and through the field of yellow flowers. At the gate Laraine would have scaled it with the same youthful unconcern that she had done on entering the property, but now she had the dog to think of.

The lock was rusted as though it had not been opened in a long time. Neal considered. 'Damn it, I don't have a key.'

'That doesn't matter. We can manage,' Laraine said independently, finding a footing on the gate. As she looked back, hoping the dog would follow her example, Neal said hoisting her over, 'Okay, I'll attend to the hound.'

From the other side of the gate Laraine watched him pick the dog up in his arms, noting that he had no particular aversion to holding it close against him despite the fuss he had made over her way of handling it. He came down on the beach side of the gate, surprisingly light of foot considering his solid build and the weight of the stray with half a joint inside him.

Neal watched him sniffing and scrabbling excitedly. 'He likes the sand.' The beach stretched away in both directions, pink, palm-fringed and deserted. 'Go on, young feller,' he said, 'you can dig and scratch wherever you want to around here, though I doubt if you'll find anything but a few old conch shells.' After churning up the powdery substance for a while the shaggy-haired scamp turned his attention to the waves. 'Looks as though he fancies a bath himself. Not a bad idea. It won't do anything for the fleas, but it's bound to get rid of some of the alley dust.'

Laraine snatched up the loose lead as the dog would have bounded for the water. 'Don't do that,' she said accusingly. 'He might disappear, then what would happen to him?' She huddled down beside the mystified animal, stroking him soothingly.

'Let him go.' Neal's gaze was on her. 'He knows when he's well off,' he said drily.

She stood up, and the dog raced for the water. He was only there a few seconds, then he came prancing back, all ears and silent laughter. 'So it's company you want?' Neal took off his linen shoes and rolled his slacks up to the knees. 'Okay, lead the way, but remember we don't all have your handy form of bathing attire.'

Actually Laraine had no worries in the water. Her shorts were brief and the waves peeled away from a sea resembling blue glass to fall languidly at their feet. They splashed around, the dog looking like a skinned rabbit in the foam, though his laughter now was almost audible as he sparred and ducked and was chased through the shallows.

When everyone was breathless though reasonably unscathed he remedied this by shaking himself furiously, evoking laughing shouts of shock and disgust from his spattered team-mates. 'What did I tell you!' Neal snorted. 'I knew we shouldn't have come paddling on his terms!'

Laraine accepted his helping hand to avoid a further showering. As they stood some distance away from the now happily burrowing animal it came to her suddenly that it was a long time since she had laughed like this.

She gazed with sad eyes at the view seawards where the trade winds blew warm from the coast of Africa, and at the distant dots of ships, and commented, 'It's a lovely harbour.'

Neal told her, 'In the old days Nassau provided good shelter for buccaneer fleets. It got rich on piracy, stripping and selling the cargoes of wrecked ships and blockade-running during the American civil war. Nowadays she's rather like an elderly lady, outwardly respectable, and trying very hard to forget her cupboard full of skeletons.'

But Laraine didn't find this amusing. She looked towards the dog and said, 'We'll have to think of a name for him. Not any old nickname just because he's a stray. It's got to be something dignified.'

'How about Woodes?' Neal suggested. 'Woodes Rogers was the first Royal Governor of the Bahamas. He led a detachment of soldiers and brought a royal promise for the pirates; pardon for those who surrendered. You couldn't have anything more impressive than that.'

Laraine considered. 'All right, we'll call him Woodes.

But we'll have to watch it doesn't get shortened to something less imposing like Woody. Never Woody.'

'Come here, Woodes, and be christened,' Neal grinned. And with a malicious gleam as the dog obeyed, 'Here's where we get some of our own back!'

They sluiced water over the sand-clogged hair and jowls. 'I name thee Woodes Rogers the second,' said Neal, entering into the spirit of the thing. 'And no letting your pals in the city know what a soft touch you've landed!'

Laraine looked glum. She smoothed the shaggy coat and said feelingly, 'It *would* be nice if he had your back garden and meadow to play in.'

'Now don't start that again!' Neal was on his feet. He looked grim as he had done when she first met him and for most of the time since, apart from a kind of benevolent uncle attitude he lapsed into occasionally, like now when he had joked around with her and the dog on the beach.

As though he preferred the grim mood he looked about him at the deserted beach and treescape and asked with some exasperation, 'Where do you come from anyway? You must live somewhere. I mean, where's your home—your family?'

'I haven't got a family,' Laraine flashed back at him. Neal saw the threatening tears again and all at once he knew that he had stumbled on the reason for the forlorn manner. He said, seeing the trembling lip, 'Look, kid, I didn't mean to——'

'I had a brother once,' Laraine lifted her chin bravely. 'He lost his life exactly three weeks ago today.'

'Want to tell me about it?' Neal said gently.

She shrugged miserably. 'He was doing some trial laps on the track before an important motor race. He hit a barrier—his machine overturned——'

'Speed-racing is a dangerous business,' Neal said quietly.

'He would never have got so keen if it hadn't been for Adele.' Laraine was reliving the past passionately. 'He was always wanting to impress her. Everything was for Adele. It didn't matter that she'd stopped loving him. . . .'

'Adele?' Neal lifted an enquiring eyebrow.

'His wife,' Laraine supplied flatly. 'She's rented the house next to your property. She's very rich. She wanted to get away from her usual crowd in England. She's come to the Bahamas looking for new amusements.'

'Bit soon after her husband's death, isn't it?' Neal said shortly.

'That's Adele.' Laraine lifted her shoulders. 'She likes people around her, her own kind . . . and especially those of the opposite sex.' Her candid blue eyes studied Neal's face and deciding that it was attractive in a rugged sort of way she asked. 'Are you married?'

'No,' came the reply.

'Engaged?'

'Nope.'

'Girl-friend?'

'What is this? Some kind of junior quiz?' Neal had become grim again, showing much of his former irritation and impatience.

'It's just that, if Adele likes you, it wouldn't matter what kind of attachments you had,' Laraine said simply.

'Sounds an intriguing female,' Neal drawled in a way that made Laraine feel flatter than ever.

She started to pat the wet sand with her feet. As though he too had things to think about Neal drifted into strolling with her beside the glistening waves while the dog trotted happily at their heels.

There were lots of beautiful shells where they walked, and Laraine was young and therefore resilient enough to forget momentarily the weight of her sorrow in the pleasure of discovery. She rinsed the sand off flowery pieces of coral and picked up encrustments of pearl which reflected every nuance of sea and sky in its glorious sheen.

When she investigated the home of a king-sized shellfish Neal told her, 'That's a conch. There are so many of them in the waters in these parts that this is what we also call native-born Bahamians.'

'Conches?' Laraine was intrigued. She looked at Neal curiously and asked him, 'Are you a conch?'

'Sure, I'm a Bahamian,' Neal replied with an odd twist to his mouth. 'Though I don't usually spend my time on home ground.'

Laraine had gathered that much. The rusted lock on the gate to his property, for instance; the unkempt weed-filled fields and happy disorder of the back garden. But she didn't understand why he was so aggressive about everything; about being here on New Providence island which was his home. She didn't know much about men of Neal's age—like Adele he was possibly thirty or more—but to her young mind he seemed angry or upset at something in his life.

Still preoccupied, he threw the conch shell into the sea somewhat viciously, then turning said, 'Come on, I'll take you home. It's getting late.'

Laraine hadn't noticed how the afternoon sun had been lowering towards the sea, and somehow she was saddened again at the thought of being deprived of the companionable feel of Neal's presence. She had got together her little treasure of shells. Then on second thoughts she tossed them down. 'I'd better not,' she said out aloud. 'Adele doesn't like mess around the house.'

They struck out along a path through the trees that like Neal's place was badly overgrown, only in this case with tumbling rose moss, camellias, scarlet lilies and crab cactus. Although the house and grounds were kept in order by those phantom workers of rented property who come and go, no one bothered with this stretch near the beach. Where tall feathery ferns looked down over pink sand and lapping waves the yellow cups of allamanda entwined to block out the view, and through the dense greenery of shrubbery and trees shone the violet of rambling heliotrope and the delicate cream of angels tears.

As they ascended woodland steps through shady areas redolent with the scent of all this profusion Neal said, 'I was here when the original owner lived here, the Honourable Godfrey Wing . . . a nice chap, but I haven't been this way in a long time.' He pushed aside a cloud of plumbago. 'He and his wife used to do a lot of entertaining . . . mostly government representatives and local officials. The place was often ablaze with light at the dinner hour.'

'It's a very grand house,' Laraine agreed, 'but Adele doesn't like it. She wanted to be nearer Nassau . . . for the parties and night life, I suppose. But it seems with all her money the agents can't oblige; not yet anyway. They say everywhere is always crowded at this time of the year, but they're looking. . . .'

She led the way now along a path which eventually led to smooth green lawns across which could be seen the rear veranda of the house, a grand structure with pillared porticoes and pink façade. Slashes of red blossom trailed around the grillework, and it may have been because of this that Laraine was unaware of Adele's presence on the veranda, although it came as no surprise; her sister-in-law was invariably to be found out here lying boredly in one of the loungers.

'Larry, is that you?' She had obviously heard footsteps over the grass and as usual her voice was harsh and complaining. 'Really, you know, you are the end! When you said you were going for a walk, in your customary footloose fashion, I didn't think you were going to *disappear completely*. Do you realise you've been gone all afternoon and there's simply mountains of jobs for you to—Well!' Her voice had changed subtly as she had risen from the lounger and caught sight of Neal on the lawn, and now in more sultry tones she greeted him, '*Hello!*'

Neal had put on his shoes and rolled down his slacks and though he was still damp and dishevelled from their sea romp, there was a virile air about him which caused Adele's coral lips to part expectantly.

'Good afternoon,' he said courteously. 'I'm Neal Hansen, your next-door neighbour. I met your sister-in-law during the afternoon and as she mentioned you were renting the property I thought I'd just drop by and make your acquaintance.'

Laraine now felt an outsider as the air vibrated between the male and female of the species. She could understand Neal's complete absorption with the woman who faced him across the veranda. Adele did that to men. She had the kind of body which suggested fragility, being thin to the point of emaciation, but not without a certain sinuous loveliness. Tumbling dark hair framed exquisite doll-like features made even more arresting by a pair of startling green eyes, heavily fringed and, at the moment, molten with interest.

'This is quite an unexpected pleasure,' she replied in a way that only Adele could. 'I'd no idea we were so close to such . . . attractive company. . . .' Then remembering that Laraine was there she paused knowingly and with hardly a glance her way she said, 'I suppose you've heard I've recently lost my husband. But as I keep telling Richard's sister, there's absolutely no point in dwelling on his accident. It's up to us to make the best of what's left . . . I mean, one has to live with the living, don't you agree?'

'A very sensible attitude Mrs . . . er. . . .'

'Really, Larry, where are your manners? Haven't you even introduced yourself properly to our next-door neighbour?' Adele scolded, before switching back to warmth for the benefit of the visitor. 'My husband's name was Downing, but you must call me Adele . . . as you're only next door,' she reitereated with a pouting smile.

'That's fine by me. I was just going to suggest the same.' Laraine had noticed that sometimes Neal's smile could be hard and it seemed to have that quality now, though his tones were suave and friendly enough.

'You must forgive the child, Neal,' Adele said chattily. 'Naturally she's upset—well, weren't we all! But these things——' She broke off in mid-sentence and pointed beyond them on the lawn to ask, 'What on earth is that?'

Woodes had come up the incline from the beach, tail wagging at the new adventure. Now he sat grinning on the grass looking like, and emanating the smell of, a wet rug.

'This young feller is a stray who has been taking our time up on the beach,' Neal explained with a grin. 'Your sister-in-law has decided it's time he had a home, as he's what you might call a tramp on the road with no fixed address. . . . So here he is.'

'Larry, not another one of your pets! Of all the things I've had to put up with in the past—it's not that I mind you littering the house with your creepy little friends, but this . . . this flea-ridden object is the limit! Of course he can't stay.'

Laraine gritted her teeth. The way her sister-in-law corrupted her name in this boyish fashion had always irked her, but not as much as it did now in front of Neal. And Adele *was* laying it on a bit thick. Also she talked as though she, Laraine, was in the habit of coming home every day with some destitute creature when at the most she had cleaned a bird once with tar on its wing, and kept a couple of baby turtles in her bath because they appeared to have been abandoned.

She argued plaintively now. 'But, Adele, he was almost starving when I found him. He's too little to fend for himself. And out here in the countryside he'll never survive in the hot sunshine.'

'I can't help that, child. You've only got to look at the thing. It must be rife with disease. I'd never have a moment's peace of mind if I knew that such a smelly unpleasant creature was sharing the house!'

Laraine opened her mouth to retort and closed it again unbelievingly as Neal said, 'Leave him to me. I'll have him cleaned up and get the vet to look him over. For the time being he can stay over at my place.'

Adele, in her clinging houserobe of pale magnolia,

looked sultrily pleased. 'That's very good of you, Neal,' she said, with her eyes only for him. 'I can't tell you how grateful I am for your assistance in what may have proved a tiresome situation.'

'Only too glad to help,' Neal replied, and taking the wet tie lead in his hand, 'Well, I must be off, I've stayed away from the house a lot longer than I intended. Nice to have met you, Adele.' Moving off, the dog trotting obediently beside him he said in passing, 'So long, Laraine.'

' 'Bye.' She lifted her head briefly.

'Goodbye, Neal,' Adele called after him. She watched him walk over the grass until he had disappeared from view with a stimulated gleam in her usually bored green eyes. She was thoughtful too, saying almost to herself as Laraine came on to the veranda, 'Neal Hansen, didn't he say? . . . I don't know why, but the name rings a bell . . . and the face too . . . now where . . .?' She came to from her pleasantly idling conjecture to carp at Laraine, 'For heaven's sake, child, go and put on something decent for dinner! I don't know why you must always go around looking like a beach urchin.'

'Yes, Adele.' listlessly Laraine went through into the house. Upstairs in her room she gazed out unseeingly at the views from the window. It was silly, she supposed, to expect that just because she had met Neal first and fought and romped with him on the beach, he should remain her special friend. And yet in her girlish way she had cherished that hope. But she should know Adele by now. She had that kind of charisma that attracted the male animal like moths to a lovely flame, and it looked as though Neal was as gullible as the rest.

Well, he had ended up agreeing to have the dog on his property after all. And he had done it for Adele, hadn't he?

CHAPTER TWO

MEDWAY, reputed to have been built for a royalist during the American Civil War, was white-pillared and majestic. Reminiscent of colonial days, it stood in grounds riotous with old-world blossom and the cool cascading greenery of trees which must have been planted some two hundred years before.

The interior too was beautifully preserved. There were carpets and gold-framed pictures from another era, and imported oakwood floors reflected ornate furniture with a rich ruby shine.

Adele didn't like the heaviness of the decor, complaining that she felt as though she was renting a section of a museum, but Laraine found the peace of the house soothing. She liked the old-world elegance and amused herself for many a long moment trying to imagine what it must have been like living here in an earlier period of time.

The main living room where she was standing now was one of her favourite scenes. A huge green damask sofa dominated and was flanked by green-gold lampshades with Japanese lacquer bases. Behind was a magnificent picture window which framed a view of the indigo and green dappled crystal sea and Nassau harbour in the distance. Just outside was a section of the veranda, the same one where Neal had stood a little beyond yesterday afternoon and——

Laraine turned away and busied herself with the flowers she had brought in to arrange. It was always the same. No matter what she was doing her thoughts inevitably came back to the man who had done so much to lift her out of the doldrums yesterday with his argumentative banter and stringent but encouraging smile. It was foolish to go on picturing him in her mind, she told herself, recalling things about him that she had been too engrossed with her own troubles to notice at the time; the way his dark hair, tumbled by the breeze, was stranded with copper in places; the air of quiet strength he emanated, despite a kind of leashed impatience in him. Their meeting had been accidental, and separated from him by the vast grounds of Medway together with the extent of his own rambling property, she probably wouldn't run into him again for weeks, if ever; so the sensible thing to do would be to forget the incident.

She had succeeded in a half-hearted fashion, pleased with the bright show of peonies and poppies she had placed around the room, when the subject of Neal was resurrected in a way that she didn't care for by the appearance of Adele.

Her sister-on-law was still dressed in a lace negligé, but there was a look in her eyes which suggested plans for the outdoors and an anticipatory excitement. 'I've been thinking, Laraine . . .' this in itself was ominous, for Adele only ever treated her like an adult when there was a duty to perform '. . . it would be nice to go for a drive and maybe drop in on Neal. Now we've made the acquaintance of our next-door neighbour we might as well further the friendship and return the call.'

Laraine noticed the way the sultry tones slid over the word friendship. She said with feeling, 'But we only met Neal yesterday afternoon! We can't call on him so soon . . . it wouldn't look right.'

'Nonsense, pet. Men like to receive feminine visitors, and if he's hanging around there as I suspect he is . . .' by her expression Adele was pleasurably recalling her prolonged first meeting with him '. . . he'll be delighted to have company.'

Laraine's instincts told her that Neal was not the type of man to 'hang about' at any time of the day. Much averse to the idea, she said, 'Well, you go. I'll stay here.'

'Now don't be difficult. You know how I hate to drive. I'm going to take a bath now and slip into something pretty and I'll expect to see you out front with the car in about half an hour . . . and, darling, do try and dress up a little for the occasion.'

Knowing that it was useless to argue, Laraine went off to her room, pondering on Adele's last remark wryly. Her sister-in-law was always entreating her to do something about her appearance, but she made no attempt to increase the small allowance she made her which had to suffice for clothes. Laraine suspected that it suited Adele to keep her almost dowdy-looking, so making a perfect foil for her own beauty, and really she didn't mind. Had she had the chance to wear any of the lush gowns and colourful outfits which Adele chose in the way of apparel she would still have preferred the simplicity of her own wardrobe.

She put on now a cotton dress patterned with tiny pink rosebuds, and polished her beach sandals to a russet glow. They made her bare feet and legs look brown and she saw through the mirror that her face too needed no additional colour, having a golden bloom from her afternoons scuffing round the beach. But on second thoughts she touched her lips with a little rose-pink lipstick.

She brushed her hair, in complete contrast to Adele's hair with its raven's wing gleam. Her eyes were light blue and ordinary too, she decided. In this critical frame of mind she couldn't know that they reflected an inherent warmth which at times seemed to light up her whole face.

Realising that the time was getting on and Adele would soon be tapping her foot, she tidied her room, then went down to get the car out.

It was as Laraine had guessed. Neal's property and that of Medway backed on to one another corner to corner and the distance by road between the two houses was considerable. She was glad now that she hadn't chosen this route yesterday when leaving Neal's back garden with Woodes in tow. It would have meant a long walk for them both and in brilliant sunshine would have been trying. And besides, she wouldn't then have got to spend that rather memorable interlude with Neal on the beach.

It was a morning for appreciating all that was good in the world, and in this Laraine was no exception. She liked the feel of the steering wheel in her hands and the smooth submission of the lemon open-topped Buick. The breeze was sea-scented, wafting from where a dozen different hues dazzled the eye alongside glimpses of coral sand. And mingling with the draughts of cooling ozone was the hot, earthy fragrance of the countryside.

Much of the greenery Laraine failed to recognise, but there were tall trees with tassel-like hangings, slender-boled and silvery-leafed weeping willow types, and crowding among them, adding an exotic touch, were the glossy fronds of the ubiquitous palm. She drove at a leisurely pace, feeling that it was an absurd hour to go visiting anyone, but Adele sat complacent, looking fragile in powder blue, a tiny silk scarf knotted attractively at her throat, and inevitably Neal's place came into view.

Though it appeared to be the only house in these parts for some considerable way Laraine would have recognised it anyway from what she had seen of it at the rear. All rambling maturity, it had nevertheless an undeniable charm being fronted by neat lawns dotted with age-old low-spreading trees which screened most of the house from view. What could be seen was of mellow brick and timber and splashes of colour turned out to be trailing bougainvillea and flowering shrubs as they drove along the drive.

Besides a garaged car within view, another racy-looking machine stood in front of the open doorway and, hating this trip more than ever, Laraine said, 'It looks as though Neal's got company. Perhaps we shouldn't bother him right now.'

But Adele had no intention of changing her mind. On the contrary, the thought of other visitors, specifically more unattached males within the immediate vicinity, only added spice to the idea. Disliking opposition of any kind, she carped laughingly, 'Really, darling, your sense of adventure is pathetic! Where you would be without me heaven knows. Still grubbing around the racetrack pits, no doubt.'

'I wouldn't be barging in uninvited on someone we've only just met, that's for sure,' Laraine replied spiritedly, never afraid to speak her mind despite her sister-in-law's inflexible disposition.

'You're much too old-fashioned, pet. Nowadays one doesn't wait for——Why, Neal! *Good morning!*' While they had been alighting from the car a figure had appeared from the doorway. In casual attire, a biscuit-coloured knitted shirt emphasising his masculinity, Neal came forward a lazy smile on his lips. 'Hello, Adele. You're looking, may I say, very delectable this morning.'

'Why, thank you, Neal. We've been out for a drive and as we were returning this way it seemed the natural thing to do to drop in on our way by. I do hope we're not disturbing you?'

'Not at all. I hope you'll feel free to stop by any time you've a mind to.' Neal's manner was suave, his smile sharp but welcoming. 'Hi, Laraine.'

By the bemused look in his sea-green eyes on her she didn't know whether he had heard their mild arguing on the drive and guessed that Adele had insisted on being brought straight here, or whether he was recalling his talk of pirates and buccaneer fleets yesterday afternoon on the beach, believing her to be no more than a child. 'Hello, Neal.' Her dress outlining slender curves, she met his bemusement, twinkling ever so slightly. Didn't he know she was all of nineteen?

It was a shortlived moment, perhaps even imagined, for almost at once he was guiding Adele towards the open doorway. 'Come on inside. It's not too early for a drink, and if you're not in any great hurry I'll get Jordan to set two more places for lunch.'

Laraine closed her ears to Adele's feigned surprise and effusive acceptance. In any case she was too taken up with viewing the interior of Neal's house. It was cool and uncluttered with a dominantly masculine air in the sparse but good furniture, comfortable armchairs and colourful rugs on the polished wood floor, not at all like the antiquated charm she had seen at the rear of the house with its carved garden benches and unforgettable stone well, and she guessed that Neal had done some redecorating and modernising in the main rooms to his own tastes.

The windows were semi-latticed and cast a mellow glow in the spacious lounge so that it was some moments after entering before they became aware of another figure lounging in an armchair beside a table littered with sea maps and papers.

'This is Stuart Meller. Stu, meet Mrs Downing and her sister-in-law Laraine. They're renting Medway, the next-door property along the road.'

The man made no attempt to rise until Neal had introduced him, and then only indifferently. He was long-limbed and slim, approaching forty perhaps, with craggy dissipated features but nice eyes which held an innate mocking light.

Adele had noticed the lack of gentlemanly response at her entry and, ever the one to voice her discontent, she drawled, 'Do I get the feeling that we're interrupting something?'

'You are Mrs Downing. And don't think because you're a beautiful woman that you're that easily excused.' Stuart Meller's forthrightness was softened only by a kind of jaded humour. But nothing could have been greater tinder to Adele's ego than this kind of approach. 'I'm a widow, so it's quite safe to call me Adele,' she challenged huskily, viewing him with the same amount of amused disdain.

'I shall call you Adele if you wish, but I assure you, dear

lady, your marital or widowed state is of no interest to me. I am a monk. It only remains for me to enter into the celibate fraternity of those who practise monastic penance where I intend to live out my days.'

'Take no notice of Stuart,' Neal grinned at the drinks cabinet. 'He's an actor by profession and he never knows when to leave the stage.'

From the sofa where she had been shown a seat Adele crossed her legs gracefully and murmured for the benefit of the lounging figure, 'I can't somehow think his advent into the friarhood will be any great loss to the theatre.'

'Television, my dear Adele, British television. Haven't you seen *The Mansion of Secrets*? or *Vivaldi's Men*?'

'I never watch television,' Adele replied distastefully.

'No, I can see you're a lady of the night.' Stuart's mocking gleam was wholly audacious. 'There's the reflection of neon lights in your eyes, and your face has the lovely pallor of too many parties and nightclub shows.'

'What's wrong with that?' Adele was needled sufficiently to reply smoothly. 'You're not exactly a cherubic example of clean living yourself.'

'It's a man's prerogative to pursue every avenue of adventure and sample all that life has to offer. But a woman is purely decorative and her place is in the home.'

'Who told you that, your sweet old mother . . .?'

While this kind of acid banter was going on Laraine's attention drifted elsewhere. She had found a chair near an open doorway and it was possible to see portions of the back garden where she had visited yesterday. There was the sound of insects buzzing around the blossom on the still air and the muted chatter and activity of servants in the kitchen. And with the sun slanting through the doorway, warm and gilding a million specks of pollen, the atmosphere was lazy and restful.

Neal handed her a fruit juice and took something stronger for himself and the others over to the sofa. Taking advantage of a lull in the verbal sparring, he joked, seating himself next to Adele, 'You'll have to forgive Stuart. A two-year love affair of his has just come to an end and he's feeling slightly cynical.'

'I've always been cynical, Neal old man,' came the bland reply. 'Everlasting love is a hoax perpetuated by reams of romantic fiction. Romance, or love again if you like, is an extremely powerful experience, but it doesn't last.'

'Are you telling us that there are no happy marriages?' Adele drawled, sipping her drink delicately.

'I know of none—except that of my mother and father,' Stuart replied after some thought. 'There's this myth that when you get married you'll live happy ever after, but the chances are you're going to be a darn sight unhappier——'

'Are you speaking from experience?' Adele broke in with satirical interest.

'Not exactly, but I've had some dreadful times with members of the opposite sex, and I carry the scars to prove it.'

At this frivolous response, Neal put in equally frivolously, 'Stuart's too wily to let any woman have him for keeps.'

'But weren't you the one who was just saying that the little woman's place is in the home?' Adele's green gaze had never left the craggy features across from her and by the taunting light in her eyes she was hoping to trip him up with his own words.

'True, sweet lady, but I wasn't speaking from a personal point of view.' Stuart slid from beneath her smiling implication with the agility of an adder skirting a prickly pear. It wasn't just a clash of personalities here, there was an abrasive quality between the two of them which made the sparks fly in a mock-humorous way. 'I don't think' he went on with his flippant gleam 'a man should have to spend all his life with one woman, that's why a lot of us steer clear of marriage. But I myself am a great romantic . . . hence my scars.'

Adele turned and with her powder-blue-clad shoulder brushing against Neal's she asked him with derogatory amusement, 'And who is this latest *femme fatale* who has driven your friend to thoughts of going monastic?'

Neal shrugged, his grin crooked. 'I'm not sure whether it's safe to mention any names. . . .'

'Go ahead, pal, I can take it.' Stuart became a tough American gangster discussing his moll. 'The separation from Junie hit me hard, but I guess I can ride it.'

'That's the girl,' Neal took up the tale. 'June Shor. She's a top American actress, a bit of a hell-raiser in the old days, you might say, like Stuart here.'

'I can't say I know the name,' Adele commented offhandedly; although this was hardly believable, because everyone knew June Shor. Laraine was familiar enough with the actress, at least by her performances on film and her frequent appearances in the newspapers. She was a tempestuous redhead, well known for her forthright statements and her talent for getting into scrapes with the opposite sex.

But Adele preferred to let it go at that. She was accustomed to being the centre of every man's universe and it irked her to find that they were discussing someone with potentially more feminine allure than herself. Skilfully changing the subject, she remarked Stuart's way with the same parry and thrust tactics, 'I can't imagine that the television audiences are actually panting for your return, but nevertheless, aren't you a long way from home?'

'Travel is my solace, dear lady. I prefer it to rattling around my country cottage in England like a pea in a can. Also I've got other interests, believe it or not, besides the female woman.'

'You do intrigue me!'

'Well, let me continue to mesmerise you, Adele my sweet, by explaining to you something of my fascination for the blue holes. . . .'

'The blue holes?' Adele said blankly.

Stuart dropped back with a tolerant sigh at her ignorance. Neal came in to explain easily, 'Stu's a keen underwater enthusiast. He spends all his time diving when he's in the Bahamas, and for anyone interested in this sport the blue holes *are* a fascination. They're underwater caverns formed milleniums ago in the glacial age. Some are more than two hundred feet in depth and many are riddled with tunnels and chambers. There are dozens of them around the islands, so underwater exploration and photography is pretty popular in these parts. Stu is interested in charting locations which might prove to be blue holes through aerial photography, and as a matter of fact we were just working out a programme when you arrived.'

Neal rose and moved to the table holding the sea maps, and Adele followed, more with the idea of staying close to him than from any apparent interest in what the maps were about to divulge. Stuart rose to devote his attention lovingly to the maritime blues and greens, and as he and Neal drifted back into talking technically on the subject Laraine approached the table out of curiosity.

Richard had been interested in skin diving and he had told her something of his adventures in the sport around the world. He had never mentioned the blue holes, but she remembered him talking about the Tongue of the Ocean in these parts and she mused over an aerial picture now photographed, the caption of which said, 'a hundred and five miles up by astronauts orbiting the earth'. It was an eerie sight, the indigo tongue-shaped abyss which plunged thousands of feet below the rest of the paler ocean floor, and between the spattering of cloud on the photograph, receding tidal currents flaring out from the lip of the abyss looked like a sinisterly beautiful necklace beneath the crystal sea.

The men had turned their attention to the photograph and Neal tapped it with a pen knowledgeably. 'There's a theory about the Tongue of the Ocean. The oval tip is forty miles across. Seventy miles north the wall slopes steeply to around six thousand feet to the channel floor. It's thought that openings along the wall let in water disgorged from the blue holes, which would explain why the outflux of the holes appears to exceed intake.'

Adele looked bored and commented with something of a shudder, 'I can't understand the attraction for underwater caves when there's plenty to absorb oneself with on lovely safe terra firma.'

Stuart was about to reply when he noticed Laraine apparently for the first time and with his broken-down debonair air he asked, 'Hello, angel! Where did you come from?'

'She was introduced to you when we arrived, but you were so busy demonstrating how the age of chivalry has died you probably didn't notice,' Adele said sardonically.

His gaze on Laraine, he looked contrite in a rakish way. 'Am I forgiven for overlooking so sweet a flower as yourself?'

'Of course,' she said shyly. Stuart might joke and appear to treat the break-up of his romance lightly, but Laraine could see by his eyes that he was deeply affected. He must have loved June Shor very much.

Turning from her with a kind of smiling reluctance, he took up where he had left off with Adele. 'The call of adventure, my sweet, the hope of contributing a little to the underwater expert's sum of knowledge, the exhilarating feeling of putting one's foot—or flipper—where no man has paddled before. All this goes to make up the appeal to me of the blue holes.'

'It all sounds terribly riveting,' Adele purred with a look which was meant to suggest that in a way she represented unknown territory herself. Stuart ignored the hint, though by his expression he was aware of it, and recognising that she had come to a dead end here Adele turned her observations to other quarters. 'And where does Neal come into all this?' she queried, gazing his way. 'Don't tell me that you too have a passion for those dark and horrible depths?'

'Not exactly,' he replied. 'I'm just the guy Stuart's hired to flip around the islands when he fancies doing some aerial photography.'

'Oh?' Adele's lovely lashes fluttered. 'You fly, then?'

'That's right, I'm a pilot.'

'A *pilot*!'

At her murmured exclamation Neal grinned, 'Does that intrigue you too?'

'Endlessly,' Adele drawled, but though she appeared to be viewing him with absorbed interest Laraine had the feeling that in her mind her sister-in-law was pondering afresh the feeling that she had seen or heard of Neal somewhere before.

'Watch out, Neal old son. When a woman tells you she's intrigued with what you do, it's more or less certain she's got designs on you.'

'What's so terrible about that?' Adele cooed, making no attempt to deny Stuart's outrageous suggestion. 'We're all entitled to a little excitement in our lives.'

'I couldn't agree more,' said Neal with his hard smile. 'And if you'll forgive the play on words, to be the source of a beautiful lady's intrigue intrigues *me*.'

Stuart rocked back on his heels and looked complacent. 'It's going to be great being a spectator for once. I've always wanted to watch someone else get flayed by the so-called bliss of a woman's affections.'

'Don't make the mistake of considering yourself immune, dear Stuart,' Adele purred. 'As I've come to discover, no man is.'

'You forget, I've sold my soul to the fraternity of non-partakers in. . . .'

Laraine drifted away from the sophisticated banter and drawn by the scent of the outdoors, she slipped through the open doorway into the tumbledown peace of the back garden. The sun was warm and inviting and there were little crazy paving paths which led to quaint leafy corners screening stonework arbours of the past. Hens and roosters scratched around the soil patches and under the trees where ripe fruit lay for the picking. There was a line of colourful washing strung between the fence post and a hook in the wall. Going by the contented chatter from the kitchen and the lazy activity from the outhouses, Laraine guessed that this was more or less the servants' domain, which would explain its haphazard charm.

But though she covered every inch of space between the house and the start of the yellow-flowering meadow, partly with a view to exploring but also with the idea of making a search, she didn't find what she was looking for. Closer to the house she heard Neal in the kitchen explaining about his two extra guests for lunch. She was investigating a wire netting enclosure which proved to be deserted when he came out. 'I know what you're going to say,' he drifted towards her. 'Where's Woodes?'

Her heart lurched at his words. Had the weary little stray wandered off? Was he once again padding along some hot country road, dodging hurtling traffic, panting for a drink? She was picturing the worst when Neal, regretting having teased her, calmed her with, 'It's okay, he's with a friend of mine who's a vet in Nassau. I drove him down first thing this morning. Apparently he's basically healthy, but he needs a few shots to make up for his starvation diet of the past. Also he's got to be shaved and bathed and deloused. After that who knows? You probably won't recognise the little hound.'

Laraine hid her relief and tried to sound politely detached. 'Thank you for going to so much trouble.'

'Glad to do a good turn for a neighbour.'

'For Adele, you mean.'

'Sure, for Adele.' Neal looked at her with a metallic gleam. After a pause he said, 'The dog's yours. When he's through with his treatment I'll bring him over if you like. Or if you prefer it you can come here and help to make him feel at home.'

'Thank you, I'd like that.'

There wasn't that easy companionship that had existed between them on the beach yesterday. Laraine felt almost antagonistic towards him, but she knew it would have been petty not to be grateful for his gesture.

As they started to stroll Neal said with a joking slant to his smile, 'Naturally the offer only applies to shorts-clad schoolgirls with a knack for arguing the toss with their neighbours and bulldozing all resistance with a kind of sweet babe appeal.'

Laraine couldn't stop her lips twitching at this, and with a mischievous light in her eyes she asked, 'Do I look as if I would qualify?'

Neal's answer was to regard her from top to toe, or more specifically her slender figure with its slight but noticeable curves in the rosebud cotton dress, and murmur drily, 'There ought to be some protection for a guy against Peter Pan types who turn out to be provocative females in disguise.'

'I'm just the same as I was yesterday,' Laraine laughed.

'I guess you are,' he looked at her closely, 'but there's something . . . an indefatigable femininity about you now.'

'Is that bad?'

She saw how Neal's smile tightened, but he queried lazily enough, 'How old are you anyway?'

'Guess,' she teased.

'Seventeen and a half.'

Indignantly she corrected him, 'I'm a full two months past my nineteenth birthday.'

'So?' he shrugged, 'I wasn't far out.'

His insistence on treating her like an infant angered her in a way which surprised her. 'At nineteen I'm a woman. You can't deny me that,' she said rebelliously.

'And where does that get you?' his grin held no mirth. 'What's so great about being eligible for anything that's going?'

Laraine stopped beside the straggling greenery of a dwarf palm. It was strange. Richard had always been the man in her life, she had never felt the need for masculine companionship other than his, but now she was fired to reply, 'You sound to have the same kind of jaded outlook as Stuart. I suppose it's only to be expected that you're two of a kind.'

'If you mean have I any illusions about marriage and falling in love, my opinions are about the same.'

'It must be something in the air,' she smiled with youthful exasperation. 'Aren't there any happy couples in these parts?'

'I wouldn't know,' came the detached reply.

'Well, I know lots of happy marriages and I think it's pathetic to allow oneself to sink to the state of believing that there's no such thing as real love—the lasting kind.'

'Nevertheless, kitten, some of us do,' Neal responded to her impetuous opinions with a tolerant but somewhat tired humour. He plucked at a leaf idly and added, 'When you said that Stuart and I are alike, there are *some* differences.'

Laraine knew there were. But Stuart was unhappy in love and it was on this subject that they shared the same outlook. With girlish candour she searched Neal's expression, his green gaze which reminded her so much of the Bahamian sea, sunny in some places, sombre and fathomless in others. She wanted to ask him if he had suffered a similar setback as Stuart, but he stalled her from making any such move by taking her arm and turning towards the house with, 'It's time we were getting back to the others.'

Laraine went with him meekly, though she was disappointed at not being allowed to pursue her line of thought, for she had found the conversation oddly exciting. She was hurt at Neal's abrupt dismissal of the subject, and perhaps he sensed this, for in the doorway he said with his strained grin before guiding her inside, 'Stay a child as long as you can, Laraine. Believe me, it's no fun growing up.'

CHAPTER THREE

At Medway they had a butler who waited on them at the meal table, but here at Neal's house things were much more informal. Jordan, a beaming native of the island, with a loose-limbed stroll and a smile which split his shiny black features in two, served such local cuisine as green turtle pie and pigeon peas and rice, while his daughter, pretty in brilliant flowered apron, brought in a basket of baked plantains, and his wife fussed happily with the bowls of flowers and fruit on the table and tempted everyone to eat more than they could manage.

They lunched in a room bright with blue-green sunlight reflected from the sea, but Adele had no eyes for the view. Her attention was wholly with the masculine company at the table, and though the conversation between Stuart and herself couldn't have been called amicable she seemed to thrive on it. But not to the extent of excluding Neal. Far from it. She spoke to the latter with a husky intimacy which at times had the effect of excluding both Stuart and Laraine, and which Neal, on the receiving end, didn't seem to mind at all.

Laraine's feelings were that they should have lunch and then leave the men to it. But Adele had other ideas. It soon became obvious from her manner that she was angling after prolonging the invitation, and during the dessert she finally got round to putting her schemes into words; subtly, of course.

'You boys must know what one does for entertainment in these parts,' she said, languidly spooning an avocado pear. 'Do you realise I've been here a whole week, alone and with no way of procuring an introduction into the social life of the island?'

Laraine knew this to be a blatant lie. Adele was rich enough to move with the international set, no matter what part of the world she chose to set foot in. Just as she had done when they had travelled with Richard to various racing events around the world, she had only to pick up the phone to find herself surrounded by the usual ardent admirers and hangers-on of the local society scene. The fact that she had so far held out against making such a move here in the Bahamas suggested that she was infinitely bored with this type of crowd. But to imply that she, the beautiful, wealthy, controversial toast of scores of parties at home and abroad, was lonely was ludicrous. But then that was Adele. And one had to admire her for her smiling and utterly feminine audacity—something of which the men also seemed aware of but were willing to overlook.

Neal pushed his plate away and stretched his legs at the side of the table, suggesting lazily, 'There's the Coral Reef Country Club just outside Nassau.'

A country club didn't sound as though it housed the racy kind of divertissement that Adele was used to, but she looked suitably interested and murmured, 'Tell me more.'

Neal shrugged. 'There's nothing much to add except that it's Stuart's favourite haunt. He'll be going there himself, no doubt, this afternoon, so it could be a way of breaking the ice, so to speak, if you went along with him.'

'If there's anything I detest it's someone making dates for me that I'm perfectly capable of avoiding myself,' Stuart said with his cynical wit. 'In any case, you've forgotten my afternoon nap. I've arrived at the stage, dear ladies, where measures to aid digestion take priority over anything else.'

'Your eagerness to take us with you on your club jaunt is positively overwhelming,' said Adele with her own particular brand of sour wit. She turned, her eyelashes swooping low anew. 'What about you, Neal? Aren't you driving out that way?'

' 'Fraid not. I've got to go out to the airstrip and take a

look over the Cherokee I've got hangared there. But I'll be along later.' He sloped a grin at his friend. 'Come on, Stu, give the girls a break. You know everyone at the Reef. You can show Adele the ropes, introduce her around.'

'As you've got me into this I don't see how I can very well duck out,' the older man sighed. But his tones were lighthearted and he added with menacing humour, 'Not a minute before three, mind, and as we live like seals most of the time at the club, I shall expect to find you equipped for pool and beach.'

'You mean I have to take a swimsuit?' Adele was wide-eyed, but game. 'But I never get wet except in the bath!'

'Never fear, my darling, there's no danger of the water thawing the ice in your veins, or is it that you're afraid that those divine good looks of yours will melt like wax in the sun?'

Laraine was breathless at Stuart's playful choice of words. As far as she knew no one had ever spoken to Adele this way before. And though he had known her only a short while Stuart seemed to have an uncanny insight into her character. It was true, though her sultry approach whenever there were men around belied this, that she did have an ice-bound barrier within herself, one which housed her own private thoughts and which no man had ever cleared or was allowed beyond. Richard had discovered this.

But far from being undermined now by Stuart's bland remark Adele, being Adele, was not short of a reply. 'No, the water won't wash them away, or the sun. Come rain or shine this beautiful face of mine will still be around to tantalise you.' She gave him a caustic, alluring smile.

The three of them smoked a cigarette each at the table while Laraine enjoyed the scent of the sea-washed beach wafting into the room. She had drifted towards an open window as a hint to Adele that it was time they were on their way, but in actual fact it was the tall and dissolute

Stuart who came to stand beside her. She had been letting the chat wash over her and was unaware that the party had broken up until she heard his voice close at hand. 'You don't talk and you don't beg for attention. Are you a doll, a clockwork toy? If I wind you up will you sing a little song and do a pretty pirouette?'

Laraine didn't know him well enough to return the banter and she was too conscious of the others looking on to do anything but reply evenly, 'I talk when there's something interesting to say.'

'And only then? Ah, child, do you realise what a boon you are to men! A fledgling who hasn't yet been initiated into the garrulous ways of her sex.'

'Don't be too sure!' Laraine laughed threateningly, because it was impossible to remain withdrawn for long with Stuart. 'Given the right subject I can chatter away for hours.'

'But it's sweet girl talk, I bet.' He looked at her in a way that made rosebuds of colour steal into her cheeks. 'Ah, fair innocence! Were I a boy again we would wander hand in hand through woodland glades in search of our own paradise. But all is not lost. Experience counts for something, and together we can discover the shady delights of downtown Nassau.'

'She's only a child, Stuart,' Adele said irritably. 'Too young to cope with your lady-killing techniques.'

Stuart sighed. 'Very well, I shall show her the innocuous delights of snorkel fishing. You're not afraid of me, are you, flowerlet?'

'Not at all,' Laraine returned his twinkling glance.

'If I remember rightly,' Neal said drily for his friend's benefit as he led the way to the outdoors, 'you were talking not long ago of entering the sacred bounds of chastity.'

Back at Medway Laraine freshened up for the afternoon in a halfhearted way. She had suggested to Adele that she should go on her own to the Coral Reef Country Club, but her sister-in-law wouldn't hear of this. 'Stuart likes you,' she had said in her succinct way, 'and I believe in humouring my men so long as it suits me.'

Laraine had gone off to her room with mixed feelings at being roped in for the outing. This was something of a new adventure for her. Always before on these trips she had been just someone to do the chores, the secretarial dogsbody and filer of appointments. But now, on a whim of Adele's, she was being dragged in on her flirtatious schemes and she didn't know whether she liked it or not. She supposed in a way she didn't mind going to the Coral Reef Club because Neal had said he would be there later on.

She didn't have Adele's extensive wardrobe nor her inclination to dress up for every occasion, so apart from retouching up her appearance and choosing a swimsuit from among her things she stayed as she was. They had arranged that Stuart should stop by at three, but it was nearer half-past when his racy machine came cruising up to the house. Laraine had been killing time baiting a pet lizard which lived in the crack of an old stone horse-mount on the drive. But it was typical of Adele to have completed her toilet only minutes before, for her tactics were always to keep the date waiting. That Stuart, in his worldly way, had foreseen this and acted accordingly was not lost on Adele. In fact it had stolen the thunder of her own emergence, for she had been compelled to wait in the doorway, and she let him know with the tart remark, 'I suppose it was too much to expect our failing gallant to arrive on time. What's the matter, wouldn't your rumbling digestion let you leave the bed?'

'Knowing how you girls like to titivate I did take an extra forty winks.' He looked through her complacently. He revved up the engine as though he noticed nothing of her exquisite backless sun-dress in virgin white silk, or its plunging neckline which revealed a tantalising glimpse of her small breasts. Nor did he make any comment on her jade drop earrings of summer viridescence which matched exactly the green fire of her eyes. He simply opened the doors and said rakishly, 'Hop in, ladies. There's a seat going next to me if anyone wants company.'

Adele stepped forward. 'You sit in the back, child,' she told Laraine. 'I wouldn't trust our Casanova friend here an inch with you in the front seat.'

But it seemed she didn't mind taking the risk herself. Laraine was happy enough relaxing on her own. She liked the island style of riding everywhere in open-topped cars and she had no worries with the breeze with her loose hairstyle. But what interested her most on that sunny drive to the outskirts of Nassau was Stuart's profile.

As he and Adele bickered in their usual satirical fashion she had all the time in the world to study it. Flaccid, lined and a little pockmarked, it was what Richard would have called a 'lived-in' face, but she found that she liked it. She suspected that behind his indolent clowning and cynical outlook on life Stuart was a sensitive type at heart. Perhaps after living rather wild since his youth, maturity had brought with it a desire for a more lasting relationship with someone of the opposite sex and that, she felt, was the reason why he had been so broken up at his separation from June Shor.

But he was still a very attractive man and she supposed he would always play the charming dissolute because he had become inured in the mould; though he had never been exactly charming to Adele, she had to admit, listening to the fracas that was going on in the front at the moment. But funnily enough, Adele not only did not take offence at his forthright humour, she actually came back for more.

The Coral Reef Country Club was part of a three-thousand-acre resort bordering the sea. There was indoor and outdoor dining and two wings of the clubhouse offered luxurious suites for guests. Docks and mooring facilities allowed for a motley collection of pleasure craft in a harbour dug out of coral limestone.

Laraine didn't learn all this until later, of course, for

their first introduction into the holiday atmosphere of the club was a rather sedate meeting with a group of middle-aged and elderly members who looked so much at home in the leather and cedarwood lounge, they might have been fixtures of the place. Whether it was a quirk of character on Stuart's part to land Adele with a bunch of successful retired couples, Laraine didn't know, but her sister-in-law was the daughter of an important business tycoon (now deceased) and she had mingled with enough of his associates in her time to have acquired a polish when socialising with this type. And it could have been that she preferred to sit serene in the glass-fronted interior rather than succumb to the threat of having to change into a swimsuit and ruin her glamorous appearance.

In any case the afternoon passed not unpleasantly. Laraine sipped at the drink that Stuart had ordered for her and listened to the general chat. She was reminded, with an inner smile, of Stuart's 'clockwork toy' comment. But then she was used to taking a back seat when her sister-in-law was around. Apart from her ravishing good looks one had only to look at Adele to know that she was rich and something of a celebrity. Reason enough for most people to want to fall over themselves to get to know her, present company included.

Also on this occasion Laraine guessed that she was too young to rate more than a friendly smile of welcome, after which she was regarded as invisible by the comfortably settled club members, who like most elderly people considered that 'children should be seen and not heard.'

But Laraine reckoned she had got the best of the bargain, for people could be fascinating, she had discovered. And there was no better way to study them than from a detached angle like this, where no call was made on her to join in the general gossip. There was Franc Kinney, an ice-cream baron from Florida, and his plump-cheeked wife Dorothea. And the Friedmans, Ted and Lonny, retired hoteliers from nearby Bermuda. Ben Woolfit had dealt in boats and his wife had done well with her own string of beauty shops. But the Bahamians, of which there were several in the group, not to be outdone, showed themselves to be equally comfortably off through some successful career, now terminated, or business venture.

One of these, Colonel Adam Webber, Laraine particularly liked. Tall and bony, his cotton gabardine suit giving him a faded military air, he had keen, humorous blue eyes and a typical drooping moustache of the purest white. She was drawn to him even more when she discovered that he was an old friend of Neal's.

Stuart had opened up this line of conversation by mentioning his coming project of mapping out potential blue holes by air, and Adele, who had already shown herself to be not a little intrigued by her next-door neighbour, had kindled the flames of the topic by constantly adding her own observations and comments.

'I've known Neal since he was knee-high to a tadpole,' the Colonel joked at one point. 'Like me, he's a fourth or fifth generation Bahamian. His line goes back to a cotton-mill owning family in England who moved to America during the Civil War because of lack of material to carry on. Don't ask me why they came out into the thick of it, that's something Neal and I always have a laugh about. But they must have made a go of it in some way after settling here, because the lad's pretty comfortably off. The only thing he needs now is a wife. That house of his is a treasure of memories, but it doesn't mean a thing to a feller living on his own.'

Adele flicked the ash of her cigarette in a way designed to draw Stuart's attention to her and remarked with a speculative smile, 'I couldn't agree more.'

Though he didn't show it, Laraine sensed that old Adam Webber found something distasteful in Adele's response. Unlike the others he hadn't been impressed by her glamour or trappings of the rich and he treated her with no more or less respect than he did the rest. But it wasn't just a coolness in him which Laraine divined now. There was something else, a feeling she had that the Colonel had talked about Neal in a guarded kind of way, as though he wasn't too sure of his ground in this respect.

She was still pondering on this when the conversation returned to more general topics. Later, having become thoroughly acquainted with all the members of the group through the various chat, it did occur to her that Stuart might have, after all, done Adele a favour, if she was in any way interested. For despite the fact that there were others in the vast lounge, both at the bar and scattered around in the chairs, it did seem that their own particular group were the backbone of the club community, and as such, the ones to know, if one wanted to feel 'in' as it were. But there was no saying whether Adele had this particular goal in mind or not.

For her part Laraine contented herself with musing afresh about Neal, and when a little later someone mentioned that he had just arrived, she was one of the first to turn her head in the indicated direction.

With his appearance—for he didn't immediately make for Stuart's party, having been buttonholed by a talkative type near the doorway—the conversation once again centred around him. Mostly it was Adele who displayed her interest aloud. Her remarks were flattering, though one couldn't have said how sincere. Laraine, above all, knew that most of her sister-in-law's observations were made out of self-interest. It irked her to hear Neal being discussed like this. To her mind Adele had a way of cheapening any relationship. After all, she had only met him yesterday and already she was weighing him up with those egoistical green eyes of hers as though he was some prize racehorse.

'He certainly looks the flier now in that blue windcheater thing he's wearing,' she mused aloud. 'I can always tell a man's occupation by the cloth—Wait a minute!'

For some reason Larain's heart, none too restful, skittered to an uneven beat at Adele's sudden ejaculation. Her sister-in-law placed her glass down trance-like and her gaze never left the familiar figure standing deep in conversation across the room as she exclaimed, '*Now* I've got it! I *knew* I'd seen him somewhere before—or at least his photo. It was plastered all over the English newspapers a while back.'

Colonel Webber stiffened visibly. 'Neal's a Bahamian,' he said abruptly.

'That might be.' Adele was not to be put off. 'But it wouldn't stop him following a career in another country. Yes, I remember reading about it now. He's the airline pilot who was grounded because of some unsavoury business . . . a smuggling scandal, I think it was. . . . That's right . . . it's all coming back to me now. There was a stewardess in it too . . . they made quite a to-do of it at the hearing. She was cleared in the end, I believe, but I seem to recall that the airline pilot was banned from flying. . . .'

'That only applies to the company he worked for,' Adam Webber spoke up fiercely. 'Over here Neal's a perfect right to do as he pleases.' His distaste—or one could say disgust—for Adele's wagging tongue was now openly apparent. One didn't have to be especially perceptive to know that all ears in the group had pricked up at her words. The cheerful club couples had arrived at that stage where life holds few surprises and though they were all obviously acquainted with Neal this was clearly a side of him which left them, to say the least, considerably bemused.

It was unfortunate that the man so much in everyone's thoughts should choose that moment to say goodbye to his friend and stroll over. 'Hi, playmates,' he joked as he arrived at the table.

'Hello again, *Captain* Hansen,' Adele greeted him smoothly.

For a split second something glittered in his gaze and then he was saying with a lazy grin, 'I thought we'd agreed that you could call me Neal.'

'But *Captain* sounds so much more dashing,' she insisted innocently.

Innocent or not, Neal was no fool. The glitter was visible again in his eyes, but now, as to appear in some way challenging and with nothing more than a look of wry humour on his face he said, 'I hope my murky past is not going to have any adverse effect on our friendship?'

'On the contrary,' she replied throatily, 'to a woman like me it only makes the adventure more worthwhile.'

It was to Neal's credit that though he must have guessed what was being discussed before his arrival he carried the thing off without any outward signs of being affected by it. He joshed with the club couples and made the ladies' cheeks glow with his rugged charm. The party was breaking up anyway. Having gossiped away the afternoon everyone was ready for some kind of outdoor activity and plans were being voiced for such things as golf and scuba diving.

When practically everyone had drifted away, the Colonel, about to leave too, stayed behind to greet Neal, clapping an arm around his shoulder in a fatherly way. They stood and chattered for a moment, but Adam Webber's warmth didn't stretch beyond his smile for the younger man. 'You're looking fit, my boy. Home ground obviously suits you'——then in the plain speaking way of the elderly he was heard to add, with a thunderous look at Adele, 'though I don't know that I care for the kind of company you're keeping these days.'

Neal, wearing a curious, lopsided smile, laughed this off with some comment, and Adele, ever the one to enjoy any kind of notoriety, and possessing feelings which, some wit had once told her, were 'encased in cement', just preened at being the centre of attention.

When the foursome were on their own Neal quipped, not unkindly, since he clearly held a great affection for the old man who had just left, 'What are you doing hiding yourself away among a bunch of pensioner types, Stu? Trying to keep out of the way of the predatory female?'

'The trouble with having close friends,' Stuart sighed as though found out, 'is that they always know your motives.'

'Are we to assume that the ladies are falling over themselves to get to know you?' Adele asked with some tartness.

'I've never gone into my popularity with the opposite sex. It's just the curse of my good looks, I suppose,' Stuart replied, making himself as obnoxious as possible.

Coming between them orally Neal changed the subject with, 'Well, the Cherokee's in good shape. I've taken her up and out over the bay and she's going like a dream. She's just the lady for the blue holes job, Stu—purrs over the dappled ocean as though she's got a special interest in those underwater caverns.'

'I'm glad to hear it, brother mine, but it's too late to start anything today. What I suggest is that we go and take a look over *Mélanie*, see if her curves are as good as they were. . . .' He left a noticeable pause, then added facetiously for Adele's benefit, 'I'm talking about my yawl, pet, my yawl.'

'Well, I did wonder,' Adele cooed in reply. 'As you've been bending over backwards to prove to everybody that you've sworn off our sex.'

'Do I detect a note of scepticism in your tones, or are you just hopeful?'

'I've arranged my life,' Adele drawled with a piquant gleam, 'so that I don't have to hope for anything—it usually comes running.'

'On four legs or two?' Stuart replied cryptically, implying perhaps that some men might play the pet dog role, but not him.

Laraine was following the rest of them to the door and coming up beside her Neal said,' Hi, infant! Enjoying yourself?'

'Yes, thank you,' Laraine replied with a forced smile, because she was feeling very flat. It would have been nice to have been noticed by Neal at the start, but it seemed that he had eyes only for Adele. It was only now when she was engaged in the corrosive kind of banter with Stuart which was beginning to typify their relationship that Neal had thought to single her out. Or so it seemed.

Outdoors he strolled alongside her where gay umbrellas bordered a blue pool and palms shaded outdoor dining tables. 'Got a pretty swimsuit?' he asked, indicating the way to the harbour.

'Well, it's serviceable,' she replied lightly, trying not to appear moody.

'Good, you'll find yourself wearing it like a second skin out here. Everybody spends a fair portion of the day in or on the water.'

'That doesn't worry me,' Laraine smiled. 'I like swimming. I'm reasonably good at it.'

'Great, but don't go out of your depth. And I don't want you tackling any underwater sports without asking my advice, understand?'

'Yes, Neal.'

'Not that there's anything to worry about. It's just that you're only a kid, unused to the high-powered selling in these parts, and some guy pushing underwater gadgets might come along and offer free lessons in such and such a sport and. . . .'

For Laraine the day had suddenly blossomed out. She had been aware, of course, of the deep blue sky above and all the sights and sounds of the sun-drenched resort, but now the gaiety seemed intensified; or was it that she, in some way felt a part of it?

It was while she was paying little heed to Neal's firm words of advice, her mind taken up with the companionable feel of his nearness, that she overheard snatches of the conversation that was going on some way behind them between Adele and Stuart. Judging by the extra dose of acidity in his playful remarks since the incident, Laraine had felt that Stuart shared Colonel Webber's disgust at Adele's recent newspaper revelations for the ears of all and sundry in the clubhouse. And she knew now she had been right, when she heard him say with soured humour,

'That was a pretty shabby piece of gossip you unloaded back there, telling the whole place what you remembered about a particular news item.'

'I do try to be the life and soul of the party,' Adele laughed airily.

'You knew you weren't doing Neal any good repeating that stuff.'

'He can look after himself, and I like to give my men a chance to show what they're made of.'

'Is that how you look at it? I thought perhaps you'd blown the gaff on Neal's grounding disgrace because he hasn't made up to you sufficiently in the half-day or so since you've known him.'

'Why should I do that, darling, when I know that Neal and I in a romantic huddle is a foregone conclusion anyway?' Adele's dulcet tones were not lacking in confidence.

Laraine didn't know whether Neal, like her, had overheard these remarks. He was still laying the law down to her about safety precautions in general on the holiday isle so that it was difficult to say.

Melanie, Stuart's yawl, had a neat white hull and gay red and white awning, and checked-clothed table and dining chairs were arranged snugly in the cockpit. Adele, in her high-heeled jade green shoes, had difficulty in stepping aboard—or was it that she wanted to appear prettily helpless? In any case, with a deep laugh in which perhaps only Laraine detected a harsh note, Neal offered Adele a strong arm for support, then practically carried her aboard.

There was not an over-abundance of space which seemed to suit the two further, and Laraine, left to her own devices, shaded her eyes against the view of hot white beaches interspersed with stubbly greenery, and openly admired the aquamarine depths around the boat.

Stuart was feeling energetic and suggested they go for a sail, and it did seem than to Laraine, watching as they glided out over the silken surface of the sea, past other pleasure craft and eventually to arrive parallel with those sugar-sand strips bordered by the most blue-green transparency imaginable, that nothing could have been more idyllic.

Why wasn't it, then? She was speaking figuratively, of course, because her flatness had returned. The sight of Adele and Neal lounging together on the white leather deck seats somehow dimmed the day. Which was idiotic, she told herself. She had no special claim on Neal, just because he had been kind to her on the beach yesterday. It was just that for once, just for once, she wished that Adele didn't feel the need to wield her subtle power where all men were concerned on the one person whom she, Laraine, had come to regard as a special friend.

CHAPTER FOUR

THE amber light of the lowering sun softened the glistening stretches of water so that the deep indigo of varying depths were like wine-dark stains on the surface. There was a languor aboard the *Melanie* that matched the hush of the dying day. Only Stuart, lazily employed in steering, had anything to say. Viewing with cynical amusement Adele's close proximity to Neal and his smiling acceptance of her perfumed nearness, he was telling them of the folklore he had learned concerning his favourite talking point, the blue holes.

'Do you know,' he said, looking over the side to where azure depths were like a circular dark pool in the midst of transparent green water, 'the locals actually believe a ghostly creature lives in these blue holes. They call it the lusca and it's supposed to be a cross between a monstrous octopus and cuttlefish.'

'They say if you sail over a blue hole the lusca will shoot out his tentacles "and once de hahnds o' de bugaboo get hold of you, you dead mahn." The holes are said to be full of skeletons of the lusca's victims,' Stuart said cheerfully.

'Charming!' Adele rose to gaze with horrified fascination into the dark depths.

'Relax, Stu's pulling your leg,' said Neal, putting an arm around Adele's waist, though there was no cause to steady her since the sea was like glass and the deck of the *Melanie* without a tremor.

'Am I indeed!' Stuart countered with a teasing look. 'Well, I was told a lusca stopped a two-master dead in the water once, and I quote, "he wrap all round de rudder and wid de free hahnds he feeling for bot' mahn on deck, den day was a scudder in de water and and bot' mahn and lusca gone." And I've heard tales of boats drifting from their moorings and floating too close to blue holes, and the lusca has shot out its "hahnds" and dragged them down.'

'That's what they believed in the old days,' Neal grinned at Stuart's mischief and gripped Adele reassuringly. 'Now it's known that it's high tide and reversing currents which create whirlpools that suck in anything afloat.'

As he might have expected, Adele was by no means reassured by these words, and as Stuart gaily guided the *Melanie* across the dark depths of the blue hole Neal seemed glad of the excuse to hold her close while he soothed, 'Easy! We're nowhere near high tide at the moment.'

Laraine for her part shared much of Adele's nervousness—it was not a very nice feeling to be sailing over a bottomless cavern with all that Stuart had told them ringing in her ears. But common sense told her that he was merely larking about; though there did appear to be something faintly malicious in his tactics and she suspected it was his way of teaching Adele a lesson for her blatant indiscretion earlier in the clubhouse.

Though it had been difficult Laraine had managed to blend in with the pseudo-lively atmosphere aboard the yawl. Stuart had taught her how to steer and showed her around the miniature cabin below, and together they had served drinks and generally made themselves useful while Neal and Adele had basked in the attention and the company of each other.

When the sea was grape-dark and the lights of Nassau were twinkling along the coast she sensed that Stuart, like her, was beginning to feel at a loose end with the unforthcoming attitude of the other two. Though his tall tales and his mimicking of the local accent had been hugely entertaining there was a limit, she supposed, to even an actor's repertoire, and in the end he said with a sigh and a voice meant for more than Laraine, 'Well, I suppose we *could* scratch dinner up from the left-overs in the fridge, if anybody's interested.'

'I've got a better idea,' Neal put in, with a zest suddenly for keeping the party at peak pitch. 'Why don't we go into Nassau and find somewhere to dine there?'

Stuart eyed his own and his friend's garb and commented, 'In hopsack slacks and open-necked shirts I don't see us getting past the first doorman.'

'I'm not talking about the plush nightlife. We could go to one of the portside clubs, introduce the girls to the original goombay rhythm. How about it, Adele? Fancy a night slumming for a change?' Neal's eyes glittered strangely but laughingly, and Adele, hungry for any kind of excitement, so long as it included men, smiled up at him provocatively, 'If you're leading the way count me in.'

'You forget, my punch-drunk pal,' Stuart eyed his friend's arm around Adele's waist ironically, 'our cars are back at the Reef Country Club. How are we going to get back home?'

'We can hire a car in Nassau for the evening,' Neal said recklessly. 'If we tie up at the West Street wharf we can be in town in five minutes and I know a place where we can pick up a Studebaker, with no strings attached.'

'Well, what are we waiting for!' Adele challenged not only Neal but Stuart too with her brilliant green gaze and her husky laugh.

Had Laraine had any say in the matter she would have asked to be taken back to Medway. It was not that she was not intrigued at the idea of seeing some typical Bahamian nightlife; indeed, such a thought filled her with a certain excitement, especially as they would have two very attractive males in the shape of Neal and Stuart as escorts. But she did not care for the idea of stringing along with Adele while she indulged in the pastime of playing one man against the other. However, no one asked her opinion, and later when she was listening to the compelling beat of the goombay drums in a lively atmosphere and colourful surroundings she was hardly sorry.

The interior of the Tattooed Cockatoo was as bizarre as its name implied. Native shields bearing garish designs hung on the walls alongside coarse drapes decorated in a similarly primitive way. Chocolate-coloured artists in gay striped blouses with billowing puff sleeves, embroidered boleros and bright cummerbunds over dark trousers beat on the barrel-shaped drums and sang folk songs in Calypso style from cavernous laughing mouths. Through the open doorways, of which there were several, allowing for the influx and outflow of wandering nightgoers, the jungle beat drifted out into the darkness and was lost in the suck and swell of the portside water.

They dined on simple local fare—conch fritters washed down with a complementary wine, of which Laraine had her fair share, no one apparently noticing. Perhaps in this heady state, being unused to the kind of high living that her sister-in-law took as a matter of course, she was more inclined to view everything with starry-eyed wonder; though inwardly she was conscious of a tiny knot of disappointment—or was it misery? She sat with Stuart at their table and watched Neal showing a clinging Adele the steps to the goombay beat on the dance floor, and decided it was misery.

But far too much was going on for her to be more than vaguely aware of this unfamiliar feeling of pain. There was the music and the personalities at the packed tables, many of them from the purely African section of Nassau, and for colourful clothing and pure high spirits there was nothing to touch them. Whenever one of these couples took to the floor everyone's entertainment was assured, as they moved with the uninhibited grace and sensuousness that was Africa.

And Stuart was a witty companion. He had many anecdotes to tell concerning his life as an actor. Laraine had to confess that she had never seen him on television. There had been no time for such luxuries in the past, for she had either been too busy attending to the chores Adele had listed for her, or in the race pits with Richard.

But Stuart didn't mind so long as he had an audience now and Laraine laughed sometimes until tears danced in her eyes. She had really no need to concern herself with what was going on between their two companions on the dance floor, yet often her gaze stole to where Neal was holding Adele close, his smile hard and white and his eyes glinting strangely as they laughed and moved to the music together.

It took no great skill to pretend that she was listening to all that was being said at the table. Not that Stuart talked all the time. There were lengthy periods when he too watched the pair on the floor, particularly the way Adele curved her slim white arm around Neal's neck, though this was not in keeping with the steps of the dance. And as he viewed them Laraine, hard put to fathom the look in Stuart's eyes, could only describe it as one of wry amusement.

It was during one of these lapses when neither had said a

word for some time that a young man with a cheeky look on his boyishly spruce features approached Stuart at their table and asked, his tones weighted with seriousness and respect, 'Sir, may I be permitted to escort your daughter around the dance floor?'

While Laraine almost choked on her drink, Stuart twinkled across at her and then replied with mock-sternness, 'I don't see why not, my boy, but no wandering out of doors, remember.'

'Thank you, sir.' The rosy-faced individual almost gave a salute, then taking Laraine by the hand shunted her forward, his eyes straight ahead. But once on the dance floor he came alive like a jerked puppet, his arms and legs waving all over the place. Trying to fit in a little with this and aware that Stuart was watching them with a benign air, Laraine exclaimed in horrified undertones, 'He's not my father!'

Her partner grabbed her wrist and swung her about nonchalantly. 'Well, he looks old enough to be, and I had to think of some line to get you away from him.'

Laraine had to laugh at his audacity and soon they were chatting together like old friends. As is natural in young people they were each curious about the other. 'Don't tell me,' Conrad McKelway preferred to exercise his clairvoyant powers. 'You're one of these rich holidaymakers living it up on the island?'

'Hardly,' Laraine laughed. 'I have a job of work, believe it or not, though I'll admit this evening I'm not too sure what it is.' Realising that her reply sounded somewhat ambiguous, she asked in return, 'What about you? What are you doing in Nassau?'

'I'm in the Navy. We're doing a charting job in these waters.'

'Oh?' Laraine had seen the ships all decked out with lights in the harbour. She had thought how romantic they looked, but there was nothing to back this up where Conrad was concerned. She eyed his jeans and checked shirt and remarked, 'But I thought all Navy men wore uniforms.'

'Gosh, no! The first thing we do when we know we're in for a spot of shore leave is get out of the darned thing.'

Laraine was amused. 'And isn't it a fact,' she teased, 'that most men join in the first place *because* of the uniform?' She eyed him critically, his waving chestnut hair and slim figure, and added, 'I bet you look super in it. Especially if you have to wear a peaked cap.'

'I'm willing to admit,' he said with laughing-eyed modesty, 'I sport a little bit of gold braid.'

They danced until they were exhausted, then drifted back to the table. Conrad by this time had firmly attached himself to Laraine. He chatted without quivering an eyelid to her 'father', treating Stuart with the same serious-faced respect that he might an older superior officer.

When Neal returned to the table he seemed to take it for granted that Laraine would have found herself a boy-friend. He ordered a drink for Conrad and talked pleasantly with him on a variety of subjects. Adele meanwhile struck her usual discordant note with Stuart, scoffing with her sultry laugh because he hadn't yet braved the dance floor and the challenge of the goombay beat.

After indulging in their customary sharp-tongued repartee he did eventually take her on to the floor. But Laraine noticed that he would have nothing to do with the exhibitionism that the rest of the dancers were indulging in. He drew Adele close to him and moved to the noisy music as though in his head it was the dreamy kind. And with Adele moulded against him there was something in his fluid style which drew the eye. It was exhibitionism of another kind and wholly sensual.

Laraine could well imagine Stuart behaving thus in one of his *Gone with the Wind* type films. But for the life of her she couldn't make out whether he was performing with his old mockery for Adele's benefit, or whether he was dancing with her like this because he wanted to.

*

The platinum sheen up there, one realised after being out in the open for a while, was because the sky was a sheet of stars. Thick so as not to be able to put a pin between and luminous enough to make the spangle of harbour lights appear dim in comparison they did indeed make a silver highway. —To what?

Laraine inhaled the night perfume of a flowering bush growing against the little porch she had discovered. She knew she was unhappy, but she couldn't say exactly why. With one ear she was aware of the diminishing sounds inside. Now that the hour was late the Tattooed Cockatoo would soon be closing for the night.

She was staring seawards when Neal came out to look for her. 'Laraine! Time we were going!' he called sharply, then seeing her dark shape he came up with a grin and a glance around. 'All alone? I expected to find you cuddling up to Conrad.'

Laraine smiled, though her teeth were on edge. 'He left some time ago. He had to get back to his ship.'

'That so? Well, I'm glad you had a good time. It's what you need, a friend of your own age, a young man you can go around with.'

'Yes, Neal.'

It was possible to hear the insects clicking in the grass over the porch wall, and to distinguish too the voiceless might of the rolling ocean in the darkness.

'What's the matter? Sulking over something?' Neal asked.

'No. Just disappointed, that's all.' It was only when she half glanced up at him and saw the look in his eyes that she knew he thought she was referring to what she had heard about his grounding disgrace. She clarified this quickly. 'I mean your behaviour with Adele. You know what she is. She certainly makes no secret of the fact that she had an insatiable appetite for men . . . yet you've spent most of the time smiling along with her as though that doesn't bother you.'

She had put it childishly, she knew, but there seemed no

other way, blurting it out like this. She noticed that Neal's granite-like gleam had returned to harden his expression and his grin as he replied, 'Listen, don't think because you're a sweet little infant it gives you a right to tell me what to do. I run my own life in my own way, understand?'

She didn't answer and when he spoke after some moments his grin was still taut. 'When you said you were disappointed I thought you were hinting at my shady past.'

Laraine had given a lot of thought to what she had heard Adele gaily disclosing in the Country Club. Though she didn't profess to be any judge of character she did feel instinctively that Neal wasn't the kind of man to let himself become involved in anything dishonest. However, not wanting to let him see that she had been brooding over the issue she said briefly, 'Your past has nothing to do with me.'

'But you can't look up to Uncle Neal any more, is that it?'

Her gaze was drawn up to his and as she searched his face she asked, 'Why are you so bitter about it, Neal? Has it all got something to do with . . . the other person involved . . . the stewardess?'

'Stephanie, you mean?'

'Stephanie . . .?' She saw his steel-edged smile glinting in the darkness and watching him she pondered aloud, 'You said the name as though it's never far from your thoughts, as though . . .'

'As though what?'

'As though you're in love with her.'

He gripped her almost roughly. 'Look, nipper, I told you to mind your own business, okay? Now let's get back to the others. It's time we were going.'

In the car Stuart, who had decided to spend the night at Neal's house, and Adele were a little the worse for drink. Companionable for once, they lolled in the back seats singing bawdy songs together. Neal drove set-faced at the wheel over the roads back to Medway. Laraine, beside him, had enough to do sorting out her own thoughts.

She believed she knew now why Neal had set himself out

to make a play for Adele's so-called affections . . . He had no illusions about her capriciousness where the heart was concerned and preferred to respond to her empty, sensual approaches as a kind of styptic self-punishment rather than think of another member of her sex—a girl called Stephanie who must have let him down in some way.

Adele was either blind to his tactics or she didn't care. What did it matter? She would get what she wanted in the end.

Laraine had never felt more dejected than she did just then. She didn't know which was worse—knowing that Neal was in love with the stewardess named Stephanie, or that he wasn't going to mind pandering to Adele's whims.

CHAPTER FIVE

THOUGH Laraine didn't get her swimsuit wet on that first visit to the Country Club there were plenty of opportunities for this in the days that followed. Adele had discovered where her next-door neighbour and his friend spent most of their time, so it was more or less certain that her plans when she rose in the morning would include a visit to the Reef.

Not that Neal was hard to find. He drove them down himself most afternoons, and Stuart could usually be found pottering around his yawl, or lounging with a drink at one of the outdoor tables. He was something of a celebrity around the club, as most people had seen him on the silver screen or on television. Adele scoffed at what she called his 'notoriety', competing with his popularity in an odd way by dressing at her most ravishing. After all, she was one of the richest women in the world, and that counted for something, didn't it?

The Bahamian sunshine was unstinting in its golden

warmth, the breezes wafting in from the mottled indigo sea, caressing. It was good to spend one's time out of doors, although on the occasions when the foursome made use of the pool Adele never got so much as a toe wet. She would lie in a lounger at the poolside looking fragile and lovely in some tropical summer garb, idly watching Neal and Stuart as they horsed around in the pool.

Ever since that night when he had driven them from the Tattooed Cockatoo and dropped them at the gates of Medway Adele had set herself out to capture Neal's attention with her ivory-skinned beauty and clever choice of attire. And sometimes when Neal stood dripping beside her chair at the pool, or laughingly leaned in close to catch one of her prettily made comments, his tanned, muscular figure contrasted in a very virile way with her slender, supine femininity. A fact which couldn't have pleased her more.

Laraine in a flowered swimsuit, bought a couple of summers ago, was happy enough splashing in the water. One would have to be half blind or approaching senility not to appreciate the scintillating pleasures of island living, and she was neither of these. Besides, she had no worries about getting wet, for her hair sprang back damp and wavy, and it was fun racing either Neal or Stuart to the diving board and jumping off with an ungainly splash before or after their super, clean-cut dives.

But often their visit to the Club was just just a starting off point for some other form of recreation. Adele had only to snap her fingers to have most of those in the higher social strata rushing to her aid. But in her helpless way she had professed an ignorance as to what one did in the Bahamas to pass the time and asked for guidance, and Neal had smilingly obliged.

They went to an out-island regatta. On that day when they arrived after a sea-crossing on the *Melanie* the harbour of the adjoining island was crowded with boats of all shapes and sizes. There was no doubt that the Bahamians were a tough race of seafarers. This was more than apparent later when the native skippers jockeyed their boats to the starting line for the race. All were rough, solid working vessels taking time off perhaps from fishing and sponging and carrying produce.

When the boats were poised on the starting line all kinds of shouts, challenges and insults filled the air. With the crowd along the waterfront joining in it was debatable whether Adele's elegant friends would have subjected her to such an uncouth affair, but she was content enough between the stalwart figures of Neal and Stuart. And as the latter was not short of a cynical comment when some boat bungled its anchor retrieval at the sound of the starting cannon it amused her to try and top his bawdy wit with something clever of her own.

Laraine, on the other side of Neal, was helped to understand the pandemonium by his frequent asides. 'You can tell we Bahamians are individualists,' he joked, an arm resting lightly around her shoulders. 'The racing rule is that if two boats are on a collision course, both must come about. But the skippers out there are having none of this. Each one thinks his rival should get out of the way, and pretty soon now the splinters will start flying.'

It was an exciting spectacle, the sturdy cargo boats racing in tandem downwind, their huge sails flapping against the blue cloud-flecked sky, and colourful crews acting as ballast on decks normally piled with produce.

In the evening a carnival atmosphere prevailed. They wandered alongside wide-eyed children under gay bunting to where free food and drink was available on the village common.

In complete contrast to this Neal took them one evening to the red velvet casino on Paradise Island just across the bridge from Nassau. It was an occasion for dressing up and Neal and Stuart looked resplendent in evening dress, while Adele dazzled the crowds with her piled high, gleamingly coiled hair-style, diamond drop earrings and figure-moulding black dress. Laraine had washed and ironed a favourite old dress of hers in lavender taffeta and Neal had allowed her to make a small bet at one of the gaming tables.

She lost, but it didn't seem important because Neal was there to offset her disappointment. He made a bet himself and won. He gave the pile of chips to her, all of which she promptly lost. But she laughed, because for those few moments she was unaccountably happy.

They went on a visit to Government House and saw its ancient cannon and statue of Columbus and its archway of royal palms. And they saw the Versailles Gardens, terraces filled with tropical flowers and historic statues, overlooking Nassau harbour, coming down to earth later when they watched conch fishermen removing the famous Bahamian conch from its shell, and vied their work sloops laden with the day's catch.

But out of all the outings the foursome made Laraine liked best the trips on Stuart's yawl. Skimming the crystal ocean was a relaxing pastime and there was the luxury of shower baths and ice cubes from the mechanical refrigerator for the drinks. They sprawled under the sun awning and had their meals at the table in the cockpit.

Adele clearly preferred these days too. The only exploring she usually indulged in was to find out who was where at the current crop of expensive parties, and she suffered the sightseeing trips with suppressed boredom, her smile reserved for her male companions. Aboard the *Melanie* she could be as provocative as she pleased, and reclining in the shade in fashionable summer wear it could not be denied she made a lovely passenger.

Laraine had discovered a fascination for the sea, partly because it was so clear and pierced with sunlight that there was nothing frightening beneath the surface, and partly because Stuart was an amusing and patient tutor. He fitted her out with scuba gear and took her down to where shoals of fish streamed by in rainbow flashes of colour and underwater gardens of sea life swayed to and fro as though waltzing in time to the gentle currents. Sometimes when fresh food was running low they searched the crystal water through their goggles and Stuart would capture some tasty shellfish with his fishing equipment for the table.

Laraine would have found the adventures wholly absorbing if it hadn't been for one small part of her that couldn't forget that while they explored like this the other two were left alone aboard the *Melanie*.

Neal had taken a critical interest in the fitting of Laraine's scuba equipment and proved to be quite a competent diver himself on the occasions he had tagged along to help her to get used to the strange feel of her outfit. But for the most part he remained dressed in slacks and shirt on deck, keeping Adele's glass topped up and lounging in a sun-chair that need not have been squeezed quite so close to hers despite the cramped space.

Laraine's view of the magical and colourful world of underwater life was clouded not by any sediment in the transparent waters but by her own continuing dejection. Regarding their trips away from the boat she had the feeling that Stuart was merely diving with her like this until he could get down to the serious business of studying what he called 'his' blue holes. It turned out that her surmising was correct, for one day he brought up the issue on the deck of the *Melanie*.

How much Stuart had noticed of Neal's smiling determination to keep up a close association with Adele was hard to say. He viewed their togetherness on outings and sea-trips with a kind of amused tolerance, and played the other half of Adele's escort in similar uncomplaining fashion, though ostensibly he was supposed to be partnering Laraine. But he had come to the Bahamas to indulge in his favourite hobby and by all accounts Neal was his key man in this pastime.

They had just finished lunch on this particular afternoon and Neal, close to Adele at the table, was lazily suggesting a cruise to Cat Island on the following day. Stuart, lolling back, dregs of wine still in his glass, put in with a cynical glance at Neal's arm encircling Adele's waist. 'I hate to be the one to prick the bubble of your current Nirvana, pal of mine, but we made a deal. You're my pilot and we've got some charting to do, remember?'

'Sure, but it can wait.' Neal dropped a remaining morsel of crab meat into Adele's waiting, laughing mouth.

'For you, maybe,' came the patient reply, 'but you forget, the bonny deep is where I get my kicks, and maybe you haven't noticed it, but I'm itching to go.'

'Perhaps his lusca is really a mermaid in disguise,' Adele scoffed with a loaded twinkle at Stuart. 'Maybe his underwater caverns are the scene of Neptunic orgies which make our little adventures seem tame by comparison.'

'I assure you, Adele my sweet, if this were the case you would be the last to know,' Stuart replied blandly, a light in his eyes that matched Adele's for challenging derision. One got the feeling that they were like two sparks that given a chance to collide would fuse into something dangerously unmanageable.

'And why would I be the last to know?' Adele enquired purringly. 'Are you afraid that with a mere crook of my little finger I might put your water-sprites to shame?'

'That I don't doubt,' he smiled vitriolically. 'No, it's just that I prefer to keep the world that I've made for myself in the dark depths away from the lovely distraction of woman.'

'You talk like a man who's running scared, Stuart.'

'If you go on with your charming incitements I might change direction, and then I promise you my mood will be anything but scared.'

'Ooh, I'm quaking at the knees!'

'But not with fright, eh?'

They did go to Cat Island the next day and Neal was extra specially attentive towards Adele, swinging her up in his arms when they beached in shallow water, and holding her close on the dance floor after dinner at the Cutlass Bay Hotel. But he was a man of his word despite his apparent preoccupation with Adele, and after that the two men got down to the serious business of work.

Laraine had come to dislike intensely being compelled to make up the foursome when it was perfectly obvious that Adele had no use for her other than to act as ghost partner while she enjoyed the companionship, though dubious in some cases, of both men. For this reason she was considerably relieved to know that the slightly mad carousel that they had all been spinning on had finally come to a stop.

But her relief was shortlived when she was made aware of Neal's proximity by his constantly dropping in at Medway from his house next door whenever his flying duties were finished. He would often call in for a drink and a chat and he and Adele would sit on the pillared veranda overlooking the sunlit sea talking and smiling together, albeit his smile was somewhat razor-edged.

Laraine hung about not knowing quite what to do with herself on these occasions. She recalled that earlier her sister-in-law had shown adamant dissatisfaction with the museum-like spaciousness of Medway, and one day she tackled her on the subject.

It was one morning when Laraine had taken breakfast into Adele's room. Her sister-in-law disliked the impersonal touch of servants she knew nothing about, and wherever they went she relied on Laraine to act as a buffer between herself and the house staff.

She placed the tray on Adele's lap now, where she lay propped against lace-edged pillows, her raven-dark hair tumbling about her waxen doll-like features so that she might have been a child; a witch child with the incandescent green eyes of a superb egoist. As she frowned sleepily, though it was well after ten, and sipped half-heartedly at her coffee, Laraine said, 'The agent has been ringing wanting to know when he can come over to show us alternative property, but so far I haven't been able to pin you down to a date.'

'Tell him to forget it,' Adele replied abstractedly.

'But I thought the idea was that we were going to move as soon as something suitable turned up? We pestered them to find us something nearer Nassau and they've moved heaven and earth'—Laraine didn't mention the colossal sum offered moneywise which was the primary incentive—'to find this town house on Bay Street. It's close to all the night life, apparently, and has secluded gardens at the back with private swimming pool and every modern amenity.'

'All very interesting, but superfluous, pet,' Adele drawled. 'You can phone up when you like and let the agent know that I've changed my mind.'

'You mean you're quite content now to stay in this "rambling mausoleum", as you called it? You're not going to mind spending your entire stay on the island in this "backwater of civilisation" which if I remember rightly was your description of Medway?'

Adele showed some slight amusement at this. 'I wouldn't go so far as to say it's grown on me, darling,' she said with wry humour. 'But I won't be moving. On that I've decided.'

Laraine's face was a little pinched as she asked, 'Has Neal got something to do with your change of heart?'

Still amused, her sister-in-law pouted from the pillows. 'Little Larry, always disapproving! When you grow up you'll come to realise what fun one can have with men, then you'll understand why male companionship is so important to me.'

Laraine felt a shaft of pain at these lightly delivered words. Old memories died hard and while she didn't want to rake over past griefs she did lift her chin and retort, 'I'm grown up enough to attend to the hundred and one tasks there are to do around here. *And* to serve as partner in the happy foursome outings whenever it's necessary.'

'That's right. I've been noticing.' Adele seemed too occupied with her own thoughts to pay much attention to Laraine, apart from eyeing her slender figure beside the bed, and noting how her small breasts gave shape to the flowered apron she was wearing. After some moments, as though the thought had just occurred to her, Adele said, 'By the way, how are you getting along with that sailor boy of yours?'

'Conrad?' Laraine spoke the name with mild surprise. She had kept in touch with the young man whom she had met at the Cockatoo that night, and they had often swum together in the pool when Adele had chosen to spend the afternoon at the Reef Country Club, but now that the visits to town appeared to be temporarily suspended she had forgotten about him. In reply she shrugged and said, 'Oh, we see each other occasionally.'

'That can't be very satisfying,' Adele murmured, shifting her slim legs under the coverlet. 'Why don't we ask him along to Medway? I think that would be a good idea, don't you?'

'For whom?' Laraine couldn't resist asking. 'Are you hoping to add him to your collection of male "companions"?'

Adele's smile curled provocatively. 'He's quite safe with me, child,' she bit into a wafer-thin slice of toast with tiny milk-white teeth. 'I don't waste my time with babes in arms. I prefer the excitement of full-blooded males; the sophisticated worldly types who know what a woman wants.'

'Like Neal, for instance . . . and Stuart?'

It wasn't in Adele's nature to look sheepish or to make a reply if it didn't suit her. Instead she countered smoothly, 'We're discussing your romantic attachments at the moment, Larry dear. I do think we should ask young Mr McKelway to drop in occasionally here at Medway. The company will do you the world of good.'

Laraine left it at that, and whenever he was free Conrad

drove up from Nassau in a jalopy he had rented to spend the afternoon at Medway. It didn't take any great imagination on Laraine's part to guess the motives for Adele's sudden interest in her sister-in-law's welfare. She was quite accustomed to being paired off to suit Adele's whims, and with Neal now a regular visitor to the house, Conrad had become necessary to balance out, as it were; out being the operative word, as he and Laraine spent most of their time on the beach or wandering through the vast estate of Medway, leaving Adele alone with Neal on the veranda.

Laraine tried hard to forget this when she was supposed to be having fun with Conrad. After all, she knew Adele by now, and Neal was turning out to be no different from all the other men who succumbed to her fatal charm. But she wished . . . she wished. . .

CHAPTER SIX

'Hey! That's the second time I've asked you if you'd care to go for a dip.' Conrad's laughing brown gaze forced itself into Loraine's view as she lay propped on one elbow in the pink sand. 'Where are you anyway? I don't think you heard a word of my description of how a loggerhead—that's a giant turtle, in case you don't know—accidentally flipped aboard our tub this morning.'

'I'm sorry, Con,' Laraine forced a bright smile. 'I was just thinking.'

'About what?' her young companion asked seriously.

'Oh, nothing more exciting than wondering what old Benjamin the butler has conjured up for dinner tonight,' she lied. 'Come on, I'll race you to the waves!'

In this way, romping and laughing with her young Naval officer friend, Laraine trained herself to put the thought of Neal right out of her mind. But then one day something unexpected happened and all her good intentions went up in smoke.

The sky was heavy with thick cloud on this particular afternoon, but the air was warm and sultry and the sea an unfamiliar ultramarine in the subdued light. Everything on the beach had a ghostly clarity and Laraine amused herself collecting shells and admiring the vivid green, motionless fronds of the palms and sea grasses fringing the shore.

It was in passing—or at least Loraine would have said so if anyone had enquired—that she came upon the gate of Neal's property. She hadn't intended to linger, but the sight of a shiny new lock replacing the rusted fitting of the past caught her eye. All oiled and neatly screwed into place, it had the look of functioning smoothly, and with the choking grasses and weeds cleared from the area the gate could obviously be opened at will now.

Laraine's heart dropped a rung lower. Of course. It could be tiresome for Neal having to make the roundabout journey by road each time he came to call. With the two properties joining corner-wise he had only to slip out of his back door and down this way and he could make a visit to Adele in a fraction of the time—and discreetly.

Laraine turned away and trudged over the sand, deliberately treading on hazardous shell-strewn strips with her bare feet in order to shut out the picture of Adele and Neal together somewhere in the confines of Medway.

It was some time later, when she still hadn't managed sufficiently to return to her old mood of beachcombing with enjoyment through the sea's flotsam, that she saw him.

Neal's head and shoulders were just visible as he walked along the path through the tall flowering grass of his rear meadow. From her place at the sea's edge Laraine could see him, but she didn't know whether he had spotted her, because his head was down and he appeared preoccupied in some way as though having difficulty in choosing a walkable route.

He slipped through the gate on to the beach, closing it quickly behind him. With bated breath Laraine waited, expecting to see him carry on across the sand and make for the blossom-strewn ascent to Medway. Instead he took her somewhat by surprise by drifting in her direction as though he had seen her after all and waving a greeting as he approached. 'Hi! I thought I'd find you here, playing shell games and garnering your little treasures.'

But Laraine had no wish to be referred to as a child. With a very adult and meaningful light in her eyes she replied, 'It's a harmless occupation.'

Well aware of what she was alluding to, Neal held her eyes, his metallic gleam openly ironical. Then he threw a look around and asked, 'Where's the young sailor boy? Not with you today?'

'No.' Laraine shook her head. 'He had to go to sea.'

Neal turned to look at her again. His gaze was different now; penetrating in some way. 'You're looking a bit peaky,' he said. 'Everything okay?'

'Fine.'

'Not still missing that brother of yours?'

'No.' It was a lie, of course. She would always miss Richard. But now his memory had become a warm and sacred thing inside her; a part of herself which made her more serene because of it.

No, this dejected feeling she was learning to live with was something else altogether. Without knowing why she searched Neal's face with her candid blue gaze in her customary childish fashion; his eyes, so different from that other pair of green eyes she knew. Adele's eyes were relentless and unrevealing like cool jade, but Neal's had the warm clarity and occasional fathomless darkness of his Bahamian seas. Laraine knew and understood now the reason for their tortured depths, and perhaps it was this that made her feel despondent. Neal was in love with a girl called Stephanie, a stewardess who had let him down in some way. Laraine's heart shrank a little. But then he had Adele to help him to drown his sorrows.

Seeing no reason to make a secret of her thoughts, she asked in her forthright way, 'Aren't you going over to join Adele?'

'Later on, maybe. Right now I've got something to show you.' As she reacted only dully to this he took her hand and said with a grin. 'Come on, it's a surprise.'

They moved towards the gate of his property, and it was then that Laraine began to wonder what the strange noises were which she had been aware of at the back of her mind but paid little attention to until now—a kind of snuffling and scratching.

She soon saw, for as Neal flipped the catch of the gate out bounded a fluffy little object, emitting at the same time a spate of ecstatic barking.

'Woodes!' He leapt into her arms at her exclamation, not too great a feat as she had dropped to her knees at the sight of him. He was fat and round like a wolf cub, his shorn hair just grown sufficiently to give him a powder-puff softness. 'He looks adorable,' she said laughingly. 'I can't believe he's the same little urchin I coaxed from the undergrowth in your meadow, but I know he is, because he still remembers me.'

Neal looked at her, at her lavender blue eyes now shining, and drawled in a dry way, 'You're not that easy an infant to forget.'

Laraine let this remark go. In shorts frayed at the thighs and her favourite old beach top she knew she could have passed for a twelve-year-old, and anyway she was too happy fondling Woodes to care about her own feelings. But dogs have good memories, and this one remembered all too well the fun and games that had taken place on his last visit here.

As he chased circles around them both and kicked sand everywhere Neal said with a menacing gleam, disrobing down to swim trunks, 'You're going to be sorry you started it this time, old chum. As you can see, I've come prepared for your sneaky ways of trying to drown me, so it's a question of who soaks who first!'

With yapping delight the dog led the way to the waves, and carried along with the joy of the moment, Laraine ran too, not as fast as Neal, who sprinted to keep up with his four-legged rival, but the final result was that they all ended up in the water, Woodes bobbing like a cork, his legs pedalling to keep him afloat and Neal and Laraine chasing him furiously while he managed to stay just out of reach. At least, that was what Woodes, his jaws wide in silent laughter, believed, and it made for fun all round letting it stay that way.

The sea under the heavy sky had the appearance and feel of green satin. There was something distinctly satisfying about splashing around without the all dominating presence of the sun to witness the nonsense; rather like getting up to mischief with the patriarchal head of the house away.

How long they swam and chased with complete abandon, Laraine didn't know, but it was she who floundered out laughingly at last to collapse in a heap on the sand. Neal was the next; gasping for breath, he crawled out theatrically to fall flat on his back beside her. Woodes, lying on his tummy doing nothing but panting delicately after the furore, regarded his fallen heroes with sympathetic interest.

Laraine turned her glance to where Neal lay, glistening and rugged-looking, his eyes closed, the remnants of a smile on his face. She was free to study him and she wondered with a catch at her heart what it would be like to have such a man bending over her, his lips almost within kissing reach as he talked. But she wasn't Adele—or Stephanie—and such girlish thoughts were idiotic anyway.

She was staring wistfully out to sea when Neal, his breathing normal again, sat up to view her. He said with a grin that was part frown, 'You shouldn't have gone in dressed like that. You're soaked.'

She shrugged. 'I often do. These old clothes dry off in a minute.'

'Maybe, but you'll catch a chill one of these days going round dripping wet. Here,' he reached for the rolled-up towel he had brought with him and shook it out, 'let's get some of the worst off.'

While Laraine stood Neal patted her dry in the same impersonal way that he had done that first afternoon when she had been forced to have a scrub down beside his well. Mostly alone on this deserted stretch of beach, she had never given a thought to the way her wet shorts and beach top clung to her young figure after she had bathed. But she did so now, and it pained her, or irritated her, she wasn't sure which, to have Neal towelling her dry like a child just lifted out of the bathtub.

While he was patting around the nape of her neck she stepped away from him and said primly, 'Thank you, but I have my own ways of getting dry. Come on, Woodes!' she called, and picking up a stick raced off with the dog in tow.

Neal, left holding the towel with nothing in it, stared at it and after her with a blank expression, then gave a mystified shrug that said, 'Females!' But his gaze was inclined to linger on the sea-wet form of Laraine as she cavorted and romped with the dog.

Later, when she had overcome her shyness, she came back and flopped down breathless, an arm round Woodes, whose lolling tongue was indication enough of the fun that had been enjoyed. 'Phew!' she laughed. 'What has your friend the vet been feeding this lively rabbit—energy pills? His engine never runs down!'

Neal, who had dried off and changed into slacks and shirt, smiled damply, 'He's young and fit, just like you. He needed building up, that's all. A crash course of vitamins has put the spark back into him, which he must have had before he took to the road.' Rolling up his towel, Neal tacked on, 'Want to come and see where he beds down at the house?'

'Do I!' Laraine was on her feet, then mentally kicking herself for this juvenile lapse she said with a decorum which did nothing to dull the shine in her eyes, 'I mean, I'd be very interested to see Woodes' new home.'

Neal dropped a companionable arm across her shoulders, ruining all her attempts to appear adult, and said lazily, 'Come on, then.'

Traversing the meadow with its tall flowering weeds of sun yellow, Laraine saw now why Neal had appeared to be preoccupied with the business of choosing his steps when she had first noticed him approaching the gate earlier. It was because Woodes, in a hysteria of delight at having so much countryside to roam in, charged and crashed around and skittered under their feet so that they did have to move cautiously if they wanted to stay in an upright position. But she was glad that the dog had no unpleasant memories of being chased with a meat cleaver in this particular meadow and happily she let him have his way; though Neal checked him sternly once or twice when he was in danger of tripping her up.

Nearing the back of the house she saw that all the broken slats of the wicker fence had been repaired, leaving no boltholes as it were, and once Woodes was inside with the gate firmly shut behind him there was nowhere he could wander off the property or drift towards the dangers of the road.

In a distant corner of the back garden Neal led her to where a newly built kennel stood out rather less obviously among the mellow fixtures and stonework constructions of earlier days. 'With a spot of paint and given time to weather,' he ran a hand over the new wood, 'it should take its place in the scheme of things round here.'

It was a stoutly fashioned home for Woodes, and Laraine was on the point of thanking Neal profusely when it came to her that men would do a lot to stay in the good books of their favourite women, and deciding that Neal had gone to all this trouble just to keep the dog out of Adele's way, she said quietly. 'It's very nice.'

Neal looked at her and asked, 'What's the matter? Don't you like it?'

'Of course I do. It's . . . super.' She forced a smile and turned away and soon the rambling charm of the old back garden had claimed her once again. She sat on a hand-made colonial-style seat and said, her smile dreamy and genuine now, 'This may sound silly, but I get the feeling that this place is full of history.'

'Only the domestic kind,' said Neal with a grin, coming to join her. 'As far as I know there were no blockade runners in the family, or bootleggers. And there are no portraits on the walls in the house of past heroes. But we were a solid family group and colourful in our own way. A great-uncle of mine used to ply a schooner between here and Haiti, and another distant relative ran a plantation on Eleuthera Island in the days before slavery was abolished.'

Breathing in the old-world scents of ancient greenery together with the fleeting fragrances of sea air and sprawling flower-beds, Laraine mused aloud, 'I can imagine what it must have been like in the old days. I bet this garden's hardly changed at all, and it's easy to picture the kind of life that went on here from what Colonel Webber told us about your kinfolk that day at the Reef Club.'

Neal smiled a little droopily. 'Old Adam's a staunch Bahamian. Like me he's the last of his line and at one time he had great plans for pairing me off with his adopted daughter. But she fell in love with a Canadian research chemist and now they're happily married and settled in Ottawa and it doesn't look as though she'll be back.'

Laraine wanted to ask Neal if he had been in love with Colonel Webber's adopted daughter, but by his detached way of relating the happening she didn't think so—and anyway there was Stephanie.

The thought made her rise abruptly. She would have gone to fondle Woodes just for the sake of having something to do, but he was enjoying a doze after his strenuous antics on the beach. So she trailed her hands through a protruding bush and smiled obliquely, 'You must be something of a disappointment to Colonel Webber, staying single like you are when he badly wants you to populate the island with your children.'

Neal shrugged. 'He still has high hopes of me producing a Bahamian heir one of these days.'

'Who with?' she asked. 'Adele? Or Stephanie?' *Why couldn't she get these two names out of her mind?*

Neal rose with a harsh gleam in his eyes and said lazily, 'That, my little beach elf, is none of your business.'

'Why?' She confronted him, sparklingly defiant. 'Aren't I supposed to know about the birds and the bees and things? Well, I do, you know. I know an awful lot for my pathetic nineteen years.'

'Living with Adele I can believe it,' Neal said drily. 'But I don't want to hear you bragging about such things, understand?' His tones were sharp and disciplinary and Laraine dropped her head, knowing that she wasn't behaving in a very ladylike way.

She went on tugging at the bush and as though adopting humorous measures to save it Neal suggested, 'Let's go and see Jemima in the kitchen. She was making cookies earlier and they should be just about ready.'

'No, thanks,' Laraine said stiffly. 'I'm not hungry.'

'Okay,' Neal's grin sloped tolerantly. 'We'll just walk.' And so they did, and after a while Laraine felt slightly better—enough to take up the conversation again more or less where they had left off. Though she wished afterwards she hadn't insisted on playing with this kind of fire, since it was she herself who finally got her heart singed through persisting in what she knew was a dangerous pastime where Neal's lovelife was concerned.

It all started off innocently enough, and the worst might

never have happened if her patience hadn't finally snapped because of yet another offhand reference to her tender age. She ought to have known what she was bringing on herself. The gunmetal grey of the sky had given the afternoon an oppressive feel. It heightened the peculiar tension in the air which somehow seemed to have its roots in her nearness to Neal.

But adult though Laraine longed to be, she was nowhere near enough experienced to recognise the signs, and so she said, harking back to the subject of Colonel Webber, 'I like old Adam. On the surface he's a bit brimstone and fire, but out of all the people I met that day at the Club I think he was the most sincere.'

Neal nodded. 'He was a fine soldier, and he's a fine man. I'll take you to see him one day. He's got an old frame house on a quiet street in Nassau. It's a typical Colonial relic; pink walls and green shutters and white ironwork balconies. You'll love it.'

'He's a fascinating character,' Laraine said, childishly pleased at Neal's offer. 'It would be fun to hear about his military adventures . . . if I could get him to relate a few.'

'Sure to,' Neal smiled. 'There's nothing Adam likes better than an interested ear when he's talking about his war career. And he likes you. I noticed that when I was talking across the room from you all that afternoon at the Club. With you an avid listener to his yarns you'll probably end up taking the place of that adopted daughter of his.'

Laraine received this lightly made comment in silence. It was ridiculous to regard it as anything but a joke, yet she couldn't get out of her mind that if she was the Colonel's adopted daughter he would soon start trying to pair her off with Neal, and somehow those kind of thoughts didn't mix with the taut atmosphere prevailing at the moment.

Jerkily she stopped by a tamarind tree and picking at its trunk mentioned offhandedly, 'He appears to have a fatherly affection for you.'

'I guess that's right,' Neal admitted with a look that said

the warmth was reciprocated. 'He guided me a lot when I was younger. To be honest I suppose I do regard him as a father, in a way.'

'Me too,' Laraine put in possessively, grabbing at something that would give her an affinity with Neal. After all, her own parents were but distant blurs in her mind and she had got to know the Colonel well on that one meeting.

Her pert rejoinder was a deep source of amusement to Neal and with an indulgent gleam he drawled, 'As the old boy's pushing eighty, in your case, kitten, he'd be more likely to see himself as a grandfather.'

Laraine's first reaction to this was to flash him a look and say absolutely nothing. But bottling it up was too much and after an explosive moment she erupted with, 'Why? Because of the difference between my nineteen years and your incredibly advanced age of thirty something?'

Neal didn't reply to this, but he eyed her keenly and as they started to walk again he said, 'You're in a funny mood this afternoon, nipper. What's eating you?'

Laraine didn't get more than two steps. '*That* mainly,' she said, tight-lipped. 'When are people around here going to stop treating me like some cradled infant? I'm sick of Adele, Stuart and you regarding me as though I were a child tagging on at a party. The only useful purpose I seem to serve round here is making a foursome so that the three of you can have your fun and games!'

Neal stopped too and the veneer of good humour passed from his face, to leave the old bitter irony. In tones to match he growled, not unthreateningly, 'I've told you before not to be in too big a hurry to grow up. Adult life is not all it's cracked up to be, I can tell you.'

'Where my life is concerned I intend to be the best judge of that,' she lifted her chin at him. 'I'm not a child anymore than . . . than Adele is,' she added recklessly, 'and it's about time . . . people realised it.'

'Oh, it is!' Before she knew what was happening he had grabbed her roughly, his fingers sinking into the bare flesh of her arms, and with an unpleasant smile on his face he demanded to know, 'What's the rush to get away from that safe little world of yours? Why so keen to be a woman all at once? Is this what you want?'

The world spun as he plunged his lips on hers, savagely, hungrily so that she couldn't even cry out. His arms were like a vice, his hands roaming her flimsily clad body. She fought then, blindly, and just as suddenly as he had grabbed her Neal let her go.

The smile on his face was still unpleasant, though it had lapsed crooked with something she couldn't fathom. Nor had she any desire to. The only thing that Laraine was conscious of was her own anguish. 'Oh, Neal!' She looked at him, her blue eyes brimming with tears, then turned and fled.

She ran through the meadow and across the sand and she didn't stop until she had reached the safety of her room at Medway.

CHAPTER SEVEN

It was a constant source of amazement to Laraine that the days could go on being so sunny and normal after the thunderclap of discovering what she felt for Neal.

She wanted to die every time she thought of that ghastly embrace, but being entirely honest with herself, if Neal was never to see her as anything but a child, or at most an emotionally safe person to be with as opposed to Adele or Stephanie, then she would rather it had happened. How well she knew now that any touch of Neal's was better than none at all.

She supposed her love for him had been growing ever since that first afternoon when they had confronted each other over Woodes and later romped with him on the beach. Since that day the woman in her had been fighting for recognition. Well, she had finally made it, and just like Neal had said, it was no fun growing up; no fun at all.

She thought about Stephanie a lot in those ensuing days. Neal had been hurt and he wanted to hurt back, and it was her, Laraine's bad luck that she had made herself a target for his exasperation.

Of course she kept these soul-shattering thoughts carefully hidden away behind a calm exterior. Conrad came to Medway when he could, and ostentatiously she enjoyed his company. And when she was alone she took herself off to the beach to collect shells. On the face of it nothing had changed in the holiday routine at the house. But Laraine had changed. She had matured in a most painful way, and it looked as though the torment would grow rather than lessen. Neal was deep in an affair with Adele and she, Laraine, would be expected to fit in with any schemes which included Stuart.

But then a peculiar thing happened, something which made the balance of the pseudo-happy foursome appear not as clearcut as was at first supposed.

The two men were usually busy until the late hours of the afternoon each day and though Neal usually dropped in at Medway after his flying duties, Stuart was too taken up with his hobby of studying the blue holes to put in more than an occasional appearance. Nobody knew why he suddenly took it into his head to arrange a party. Being Stuart, and enjoying the adulation that an actor takes as a matter of course, it was probably second nature to him to want to bask in the limelight occasionally despite, or perhaps because of, his diving mania.

In any case a table was booked for four at the Carib Club in Nassau, a dining and dancing night spot on West Bay Street. Then at the last minute Stuart had technical problems aboard the *Melanie*, about to anchor after a diving expedition. The three of them were dressed and ready to start out when the news came that Stuart might not be able to get to the party after all. But Neal decided to make for the Carib Club anyway.

That was how Laraine came to be seated in the back of his car attired in one of her few evening dresses, a simple cocktail-length pink silk with a velvet sash at the waist. Adele looked beautiful in an evening creation of coffee-cream satin and an elaborate hair-style devised by a hairdresser who had been summoned to Medway. Neal, seated next to her at the wheel, was his usual pleasant withdrawn self, but ruggedly attractive, to Laraine at least, in evening dress.

On the occasions when she had run into him at the house he had given no sign that he remembered anything of that brutal embrace she had let herself in for that afternoon in his garden. And likewise she pretended that it was one of those crazy incidents that fade just as quickly from the mind. But inwardly she longed to feel the touch of his hand encompassing hers, if only like when they had raced towards the waves together.

She would have been grateful for anything at all that would have indicated his awareness of her. But this, she supposed, was a pretty futile hope. What could she expect with the dangerously lovely Adele always at his side? The subtle yet lustful charms of her sister-in-law suited the grimly smiling Neal admirably, for with Adele he need give nothing of himself as he obviously had done with Stephanie, with disastrous results.

The bright lights of the Carib Club helped to focus attention on the stunning entrance of Adele on Neal's arm. She enjoyed the acclaim reserved for only the top socialites in this stratum of society, and Neal carried it off with the ease derived no doubt from his years as an airline pilot, most of whom are expected every once in a while to put in an appearance at such gatherings.

Laraine kept to the shadows wherever she could, wishing

fervently that she could be transported to the palm-fringed isolation of her favourite haunt, the beach, but torn in two with a desire also to stay near Neal and glean what she could for her recently awakened heart from his expressions.

When the admiration had died down and everyone had returned to the all-absorbing business of enjoying themselves, the three of them dined in comparative privacy at a centre table from a menu which consisted of cracked conch in hot sauce with barefoot rice, guava salad, and island fruits and wine.

The music was an ever-pleasant background and as the evening progressed dancers took to the floor. It began to look as though the empty chair at a certain centre table was going to remain empty. Her inner self achingly conscious of Neal's presence, Laraine had forgotten all about Stuart. But it appeared that Adele hadn't. There was no saying what prompted Laraine to glance across the table at the same moment that a tall figure could be seen making his way across the room. But look she did, and it was the breathless expression on Adele's face that shook her; the ardent, leaping light bared for several palpitating seconds in those green eyes as Stuart made his way to their table, which caused Laraine to bite on her lip in silent surprise.

It was as though she had imagined it, however, for on Stuart's arrival Adele's greeting was more biting than ever. 'Well, look what the tide's washed up! It looks as though the dashing yawl skipper has given his *Melanie* the brush-off for once, in favour of our unexalted company.'

'You do yourself an injustice, my dear Adele.' Stuart as always exquisitely unruffled bowed chivalrously over her hand. 'Half the room have eyes only for you, and the other half would be only too ready to lick those pretty evening sandals of yours—*and* you know it.'

Adele smiled at him, making the most of the attention they were attracting from the other tables, and replied ignominiously, 'Is that why you've come? To steal some of my thunder?'

'Unlike you, my sweet, my popularity doesn't depend on how many dollars I have in my account. There's a little thing called talent which far outweighs beauty and a string of noughts after every digit at one's bank.'

'You *did* say a little thing!' Adele, never at a loss for a carping rejoinder, twisted his words mockingly. Though she was determined to ignore the fresh murmur of approbation circulating among the tables it was fairly obvious that Stuart, tall and attractive in a rakish way, and above all a star, was the cause of this new commotion.

It hadn't altogether died down when later Stuart took Adele on to the dance floor, and as he moved in the charmingly dated way of his, holding Adele with a threatrical passion which she at least appeared to have no objection to, the non-dancers watched enraptured, reading romance in every gesture of the moulded couple.

Herself an onlooker, Laraine couldn't help thinking wryly that unknown to the adoring public the pair were probably flaying each other with smilingly corrosive tongues; though she hadn't forgotten that look she had seen in Adele's eye, albeit it had been a swiftly passing thing.

Busy with her own thoughts, she was still acutely conscious of being alone at the table with Neal. The recent awakening in her had brought with it a terrible shyness where he was concerned, and when he finally asked her to dance she accepted with a mixture of dread and soaring happiness.

She felt stiff and awkward held against him and he moved in a withdrawn way as though making the most of the tropical-sounding music and general carefree atmosphere of the place. The laughing intimacy they had shared on the beach seemed to belong to another world, but then he began to chat and miraculously her shyness dissolved and she became supple in his arms.

'Woodes is missing you no end,' he said, shielding her

from an elephantine couple with John Travolta aspirations. 'I told him you'd come and see him every day and so far you haven't turned up once.'

The question of cutting herself off from the little dog had been a deep source of unhappiness with Laraine, but how could she gaily make visits to the house next door knowing now how she felt about Neal? Hedging, she said, 'I wasn't aware that the invitation to see him settled in was a permanent one.'

'What else would it be?' Neal shrugged. 'Woodes is your dog and you can't have him at Medway, so the logical answer is for you to come and see him at my place.'

Laraine didn't know why she should visualise at that moment the well-oiled fastening on the gate of Neal's property; and come to think of it he had continued to make his visits to Adele at Medway by car despite the easy access by the beach. Could it be that he had fixed the gate so that she, Laraine, could use the meadow for the purposes of dropping in on Woodes? Or was she being wildly imaginative to even consider such a thing?

There was no saying whether he knew something of her thoughts or not, but with an odd gleam in his eye he added, 'I was going to tell you to feel free to look in on your canine pal any time, but you scooted away so fast that afternoon there was no time to make any such formal invitation.'

Laraine swallowed with difficulty. This was another matter. This was the incident, obliquely alluded to, which remained engraved on her mind, and it appeared that Neal hadn't forgotten it as he had led her to suppose.

She said, giving him a straight look, 'I seem to recall there was a definite reason why I scooted, as you call it, off your property that day.'

He had the grace to look sheepish, but there was a hard twinkle in his eye as he shrugged, 'You wanted to grow up. I gave you a helping hand, that was all.'

'Thank you for the experience,' she said unsmilingly. 'I'm sure I shall find it invaluable.'

'My advice is to stay in your little-girl world, kitten,' he said, tightlipped. 'Come out of it and you're liable to get hurt.'

'And you're such an authority on the subject, after all!'

Her mocking reply did not amuse Neal. 'You're talking much too sophisticated for that young head of yours,' he said grimly. 'Let's dance.'

They didn't chat any more. The antagonism that had built up between them made Laraine miserable, and Neal was inclined to hold her aggressively close.

How much that aggressiveness had to do with what followed later there was no saying. All Laraine knew was that if she had been miserable before, she was desolate when she heard Neal and Adele make a pact to opt out of the general living on New Providence and take off together somewhere for a remote isle.

It could have been something to do with that look she had seen in Adele's eye earlier. There was not a trace of it now and her manner towards Stuart was derisive, almost vicious. That was when she condescended to pass the time of evening with him, for as they all sat at the table with drinks after the dancing her attention was mainly with Neal. But that didn't stop her making remarks alluding to the other male member of the party, a favourite trick of hers, as was the case when she said at one point, 'We seem to spend all our time playing second fiddle to a super she-craft afloat these days. It's refreshing to know that your Indian maiden of the skies doesn't rule you entirely, Neal. The Piper-Cherokee, don't you call it?'

'That's right,' Neal nodded. He added with a grin, 'You'll have to take a flip with me some time. The view from up there over the islands will take your breath away.'

'I might just do that,' said Adele with a recklessness that was not in keeping with her usual smooth self-assurance. She went on to say, 'Private flying is not new to me, you know. I used to run a club jet, but it was lying idle most of the time and I found the upkeep too costly.'

'This is not jet travel,' Neal told her, warming to his subject, 'and for that reason it's infinitely more enjoyable. I swear you can see Stuart's mermaids and a lot more than you would notice in a glass-bottomed boat, flying a few feet above the waves.'

'Well, what are we waiting for?' Adele's laugh had a brittle sound. 'When do we leave—and come to think of it, why don't we make it a real trip? You can take me to some desert island and we'll go native for a while. How's that?'

For forced gaiety Neal's mood was not far short of matching Adele's as he glanced questioningly across the table. 'We'll have to ask the boss. Unfortunately Stu's booked my time, and a deal is a deal.'

'If you're bent on taking up the lady's suggestion,' Stuart said drily, reaching for a leisurely sip of his drink, 'I can spare you for a couple of days. I'm thinking of taking a break myself over at Cat Cay, so feel free, old son.'

Adele sought fit then to address her next remark pointedly his way. 'And who do you know on the private island luxury resort of Cat Cay?' she asked with her usual barbed sweetness.

'Oh, I have my friends, darling,' Stuart responded in like tones. And with a challenging gleam in his rakishly smiling eyes he invited, 'You're welcome to come and share my luxury paradise if the idea appeals.'

'I've made my date, thanks.' Adele's eyes smouldered their reply, giving one the feeling that she was fighting a powerful urge inside to fall in with Stuart's suggestion. And with a new burst of recklessness which to Laraine's mind held a note of desperation she laughed, 'Neal and I know how to enjoy ourselves. Isn't that right, Neal?'

'You bet!' His arm tightened about her slender waist and his smile was tightly sloping and indulgent, and Laraine wanted to die.

It was easy to become lost in the polished spaciousness of Medway. Though Laraine had grown quite attached to the majestic old house she had to admit that without Adele it was a pretty lonely place.

She hadn't been around when Neal had called. She had packed her sister-in-law's overnight bag and from her room she had heard this being stowed into the car. Later the pair had driven away and Laraine was left alone to battle with an overwhelming despair.

At first she wished that Conrad had been around to allay some of this colossal loneliness, but then she realised it would have been worse trying to put on a carefree air when her heart was a lead weight inside her, and anyway her young Naval officer friend was working at sea.

She strolled over to see Woodes and though the little dog went into ecstasies at the sight of her and made a boisterous playmate in the meadow and on the beach, the blue of the sky and the loveliness of the palm-fringed shore was lost on her, for the breeze and the gentle lapping of the waves had only one thing to say to her: *Adele and Neal, Adele and Neal. . . .*

Without the smiling, forceful presence of Neal to tease and splash with her, the beauty of the day was a new pain in her heart, so she took Woodes back to his paddock and returned to the house where everything was blacker still.

She wasn't sure when it was that Stuart called. Time had ceased to have any significance for her. She was dully going about the business of tidying up Adele's room when she heard his car outside on the drive.

She went down to find him drifting towards the open doorway looking very debonair in white flannels and blazer. 'Why, Stuart!' She didn't bother to hide her surprise at his appearance. 'I thought you said you were going to Cat Cay?'

'I'm on my way,' he nodded towards his holiday gear in the back of the car. 'Just thought I'd stop by and see how things were at Medway.' He cast a casual glance around the empty hall and driveway and added laconically, 'So the honeymoon couple have departed.'

Laraine endeavoured to reply naturally, though inwardly the gloom deepened at his description of Neal and Adele. 'Oh yes, they left first thing this morning.'

Stuart didn't seem to pay much attention to her bright answer. Looking at her from where the sunlight was softening his craggy, good-looking features through the doorway, he asked, 'What are you going to do with yourself for the next couple of days?'

'I hadn't really thought about it,' Laraine shrugged as if this was a minor detail.

'Just as I gathered,' Stuart nodded as though to himself, 'that lovely, selfish sister-in-law of yours has left you to rub along the best you can while she indulges her whims elsewhere.'

'I wouldn't say that.' Laraine made an effort to appear brisk. 'In actual fact I've got lots to do. There's quite a bit of paperwork to catch up on—Adele's bills mostly—and I might make a trip to town, several of her outfits need cleaning. . . .'

'I've got a better idea,' Stuart broke in. 'Why don't you come with me to Cat Cay?'

'With you?' Laraine was completely bowled over by the suggestion. 'I couldn't do that,' she laughed shakily.

'Why not? Doesn't the idea of sugar-pink cottages on a dazzling white beach and dinner in an eighteenth-century manor house do anything for you?'

'Of course,' Laraine admitted, 'but I'm no match for your sophisticated friends, Stuart, and besides, I don't have the clothes. . . .'

He eyed her quizzically and asked with a dissipated gleam, 'Afraid to spend the night with the big bad Romeo?'

'Not in the least,' Laraine replied smilingly. In name he might be the island's most disreputable womaniser, but she had long suspected that it was just another part he played to disguise his real feelings.

'All right, nip upstairs and chuck a few things into a bag

and let's be on our way,' he said with a grin. 'Cat Cay is beckoning and for once we don't have to work aboard the *Melanie* to get there.'

Because of the similarity in the names Laraine had undoubtedly been confusing their destination with Cat Island, east of Nassau. She hadn't realised that it would mean an air trip and that Cat Cay was all of a hundred and fifty miles from New Providence Island. If she had she might not have been so ready to accept Stuart's invitation. It had seemed a good idea to get away from the bleakness of Medway without Neal around, but sitting in the sturdy aircraft operated by Bahamas Airways she realised that the bleakness was still with her and that there was no escaping the fact that Neal had gone away with Adele; flying like this. Not, however, in the impersonal atmosphere of public transport. No, it was cosily just the two of them in Neal's light plane and they could touch down wherever the mood took them. And what a wealth of spots to choose from in an area which hadn't changed much from the old days and was still littered with romantic desert islands!

It was no use denying that such thoughts were sheer torment to her recently awakened emotions, but she was young enough to feel a certain excitement at seeing new places and Stuart was an entertaining companion. And while inwardly the miserable ache could not be forgotten, outwardly she had enough to occupy her as a means of ignoring it.

Cat Cay was all of how Stuart had described it to her and more. There truly were pink and white cottages on a virgin strip of beach, but he hadn't said anything about the saphire blue of the Gulf Stream outside their front door, or the dazzling views framed by palms on this delectable edge of the tropics.

They picnicked in the flower-strewn plot fronting their cottage and swam where the depth of blue must surely leave a stain on them, Laraine thought, only to discover that once afloat the sea's clarity had never been more stunning.

That they never saw a soul all afternoon was perhaps due to the tennis courts and skeet range and other sports amenities designed to relieve the boredom of the idle rich.

The one thing that Laraine liked about Stuart was that he treated her as an equal. He talked to her as though she was mentally, if not age-wise, on a level with him, and apart from that first meeting when he had teased her outrageously he never made reference to her youth like Neal did. She could have been Stuart's daughter, but he was ageless and debonair in this respect and the idea was ludicrous. She didn't see him as a family man, on the other hand he didn't consciously try to make her aware of his vast experience with women, and for this reason she found him curiously restful to be with. It seemed there, at Cat Cay, as if he had discarded completely his role of the jaded lover, and the atmosphere was one of near contentment and relaxation.

Laraine did admit, however, to some slight feeling of trepidation when evening came and she was faced with the prospect of meeting Stuart's affluent friends over dinner at the Manor House. She was not entirely ignorant of these occasions, having attended quite a few such events with Adele and Richard, when he was alive, but out here on a private luxury island where the only guests were hallowed club members or their associates, it was all something of an unknown quantity for her.

As it happened the evening couldn't have gone more smoothly. Stuart, possessing that indefinable charisma which many actors enjoy, was received with enthusiasm wherever he went, and tonight was no exception. Laraine did feel herself being eyed rather curiously while Stuart was bombarded with amused, knowing glances as he escorted her among the party couples taking pre-dinner drinks. But she had little to do really except listen to the sophisticated conversation, spiced by Stuart's cynical wit, and with everyone formally dressed she felt that she just scraped by in her much worn pink silk.

After the banquet which was modestly described as dinner Stuart bowed out of such masculine activities as knocking a ball round in the billiard room, or relaxing with a cigar in the panelled library which, like the rest of the Manor House, had been transported brick by brick from England, and with his arm in Laraine's he led the way back to their beach cottage.

The moon gilding the tranquil ocean gave it an oyster satin serenity, and the white sand was toned down to a dusky ivory under the stars. Stuart looked ill at ease in his evening dress and tugging at his bow-tied collar he asked, 'Fancy a swim before bed?'

'I'd love one,' Laraine laughed, only too eager herself to get out of the claustrophobic confines of her dress. Cat Cay, despite its luxurious trappings, was a place where one lived close to nature, and nothing could have been more the case as the two of them, clad only in swimsuits, basked in the shallow waves under star-washed heavens.

Laraine had made a pact with herself not to think about Neal, but it was moments like these when the awful, miserable truth engulfed her and there was no shutting out of her mind the picture of him alone with Adele in a spot even more idyllic than this.

Perhaps because of this she swam too long and became somewhat chilled, and Stuart had to lend her his warm beach robe and make hot drinks which they sipped companionably on the doorstep of the cottage.

It was a night for letting one's thoughts drift. The scent of flowers from the little garden patch mingled with the breath of the sea and the left-over warmth of the sand. Beyond the pewter glow of the horizon stretched infinity. After a while Stuart said, musing aloud at the peace, 'It's hard to believe that the noise and glitter of Miami Beach is only about fifty miles away.'

'Are we so near the American coast?' Laraine stirred herself to exclaim, then lapsing back into the comfortable niche of just idling she asked, 'Do you know Florida at all?'

'I've been there a few times,' Stuart nodded. 'But California is the place we actors usually make for.'

'They say there are almost as many British living there now as there are Americans,' Laraine smiled. 'Is that right?'

Stuart nodded. 'Television has a lot to do with it. If an actor or an actress can get into one of these big block-buster serials they're more or less made, and they usually end up buying a plush villa round Beverly Hills way and settling there.'

'Have you never wanted to do that?' Laraine queried, hugging his beach robe round her.

'I wouldn't be fooling myself or anyone else if I said I wasn't interested in such work,' Stuart stretched his long legs. 'But it can be tricky. The one thing an actor has to guard against is becoming type-cast. If your face fits too well into the part and sticks in the mind of the public no producer will touch you. I know quite a few in my profession who have been out of work for a very long time through playing the same character for too long on the box.'

'And yet in these latest American sagas we see the same stars popping in and out in different roles.' Laraine had never had time to become an avid T.V. fan, but this much she had noticed.

'True,' Stuart acknowledged. 'But even a star can make the mistake of becoming over-exposed.' His smile became a little nostalgic. 'I had a meaty part in one of those sagas some time back. That's where I met June.'

'June Shor, the girl you were in love with?' Laraine was suddenly more wide-awake. Giving him a sideways look in the moonlight, she asked, 'Or is it incorrect to talk in the past tense?'

Stuart gave one of his customary cynical replies. 'What is love anyway but a hankering after the flesh? And there's lots of that around.'

Had it been anyone else Laraine might have been shocked by this reply. But she knew Stuart too well by now not to take his every word seriously, and staring to where the waves were folding themselves on the moonlit beach she said softly, 'I don't think you believe that any more than I do.'

He gave a kind of mirthless laugh. 'No, that's rubbish and we all know it. When you find the right person bed is an essential part of the partnership, but there's a mental fusing as well so that whatever you do together, any little old thing like boating in the park or cooking spaghetti bolognaise, or debating over what's caused a fuse—whether you're getting all the breaks or going through a crisis, you know there's no one else you'd rather be doing it with.'

Laraine was silent for a moment, then she said intuitively, 'You must have got to know June very well.'

'We lived together for two years—through the fights and scandals—and ecstasies.' Stuart spoke reminiscently. 'June's quite a bit younger than me. In the old days she liked the idea of me sheltering and protecting her, but she's come a long way since then. She's learned to spread her wings and become her own person, and though I wish her well I miss the old Junie.'

'If you felt like that about her why didn't you marry her when you had the chance?' Laraine asked.

'Our types are more inclined to run a mile rather than take advantage of any opportunity to seal our fate completely. We like everything open-ended, so that there's at least one bolthole should things get rough.' Stuart's grin was lopsided as he looked at her. 'I can see you're one of those who don't believe in such relationships.'

'No, I don't think I do,' Laraine said thoughtfully. 'To me it seems as though there's a selfishness on both sides; a holding back of some vital part that neither is prepared to relinquish in the selfless act of marriage. If you're not prepared to give all how can any partnership work out?'

'We're all selfish to a certain degree, I'll admit.' Stuart shifted and grimaced humorously. 'Like now, for instance. My creaking bones are playing up after the run-around you've given an old-timer like me, wearing me out with your beach and water games. I'm going to pack you off inside and fetch one of the sleeping bags out here and try to recover enough stamina for a round of golf tomorrow.'

Laraine laughed, knowing that for the most part he was joking, but once she was between the sheets listening to the muffled whisper of the surf she went over in her mind all that he had told her about June Shor. And curiously Stuart's pining for something he couldn't recapture made her love for Neal seem an infinitely more precious, though agonising thing.

CHAPTER EIGHT

WHILE Stuart roamed with his friends the next day, over the golf course in the centre of the island, Laraine passed the time arranging a special lunch table. She picked brilliant flowers from the beach cottage garden and a sprig of delicate blossom, which made the makeshift table she had fixed up in the sand appear gay and festive.

She had shopped at one of the fresh fish stalls which served the villa owners on the island, and though she didn't know a great deal about the preparation of Bahamian-style seafood it all turned out rather well. On a luxury island of this sort there was no need of course to lift a finger; at least only to press a bell in the cottage which would have summoned waiter service and a full-scale meal elaborately laid out. But work helped to blot out the picture of Neal and Adele in each other's arms somewhere, and Laraine contrived to keep busy long after Stuart, highly amused at the rustic tea party, had eaten his fill and sprawled to take a nap in one of the beach loungers.

They had originally planned to leave at six, but a chance visit to an adjoining cottage where a cocktail party was in full swing prolonged their stay considerably, so that it was after nine when they finally took off in the plane that would carry them back to New Providence Island. Laraine made the return trip with mixed feelings. She had missed Neal desperately, but she wasn't looking forward to meeting him again knowing that he had been away on a secret trip with Adele.

If the truth were known she was feeling utterly miserable; worse now than when she and Stuart had started out. It didn't seem possible that she could experience any greater desolation than this—but that was before they had covered the last few miles from Nassau by road and finally entered the approach to Medway. When Laraine saw Neal's car still parked in the driveway, though it was now the early hours of the morning, her spirits had never been lower.

The odd thing was that neither party seemed greatly aware of the other's presence in the subdued lighting of the interior. When she and Stuart entered the room with the picture window looking out on to the now shrouded night, Adele was standing near the mantelpiece, one hand stretched out for support, the knuckles of which were white as it gripped the lip of the marble surround. There was a strange brilliance in her green eyes and her flaring nostrils marred considerably her usual flawless beauty.

It was Neal who spoke. From his place beside one of the settee side tables he lowered the photo frame he had been idly fingering and said in tones laced with sarcasm, 'So the prodigal pair have decided to return. I'm afraid you've missed supper, but in a short while now we should all be able to sit down to breakfast.'

Stuart grinned affably and explained, 'We would have been back sooner, but I ran into Jack Simmons over a last-minute drink, and you know how these actors agents can spout.'

'No, I don't. It's not my line of business,' said Neal with

a kind of ominous calm. There was a white line around his lips which smiled in an odd way as he remarked, 'Benjamin told us you'd both taken off for Cat Cay, but as I recall you said nothing about including Laraine in your flip towards the Florida coast.'

'Last-minute thought, old man,' Stuart shrugged. 'I happened to be passing and decided to stop off to see how things were——'

'Don't give me that, Meller,' Neal cut in with that same brutal calm. 'Medway is nowhere near the route to the airport from your hotel and we both know it.'

'All right.' Stuart's face clouded over, possibly with annoyance. 'So I made a special trip out here. And why not? You two couldn't care a hang about a kid left here in this beachside castle with only a grizzled butler for company, but I can tell you it bothered me no end.'

'Any excuse to take advantage of a lone female,' Neal sneered. 'You never get tired of playing the virile charmer, do you, Meller? The answer to a woman's prayer.'

'You're not doing too badly yourself.' Stuart made the oblique reply, his own face now a mask of suppressed anger.

'What I do I keep within the bounds of decency,' Neal said quietly, the white line around his mouth more pronounced. 'So far as I know, no one has ever accused me of child-snatching.'

'Nor me,' Stuart retorted almost flippantly. 'Laraine is a very delectable piece of womanhood and I was only too pleased to show her the sights of Cat Cay.'

'Oh, sure! You're the greatest guide in the business, but I seem to remember that bedrooms are your real speciality, particularly those in lonely beach cottages with not a soul for miles.'

'You've got it wrong. The place was absolutely flourishing with people. As a matter of fact we went for dinner in the Cat Cay Manor House and you couldn't move for guests. Laraine had a ball listening to the racy chat.'

As though in an attempt to cool his own rising temper as well as the somewhat inflammatory atmosphere Stuart resorted to placatory tones. But Neal remained white-lipped. 'And what then?' he snapped. 'I suppose you saw to it that she was tucked up in one of the Manor bedrooms for the night?'

'Well, no, not exactly. . . .'

'No? Yet you were on just now about her being just a kid left to fend for herself at Medway.'

'I'll admit she's a little inexperienced. . . .'

'Exactly. And I won't have you fouling up her young life with your loose ways, understand?'

'Hold it, Neal. Ho . . . ld it!' All Stuart's intentions to stay peaceable evaporated in that moment. His eyes glinting darkly, he said, 'If you'll cast your mind back you'll also recall that it's me who's supposed to be on the waggon where women are concerned. And if there's any lowering of morals and tainting of young minds with unsavoury conduct you want to take a look at yourself——'

'I haven't yet abducted a child and spirited her——'

'*Now wait a minute!*' As Laraine stepped into the argument both men's heads swung round. Her usually docile blue eyes blazing in her small face, she took the floor. 'There's something we've got to get straight. For one thing. I'm nineteen years old and by today's standards that makes me an adult. And just because you all consider yourself so superior and mature it doesn't alter the fact that anywhere else I would be considered an old hand at all this dating and lovemaking you think you're so expert at.

'And another thing, I don't need anyone's protection. I grew out of that years ago. I certainly am not at a loose end if I'm left on my own for a while, nor will I be told how to run my life. I shall go where I like with whomever I please, and the sooner you all drop the idea that you've got an infant in your midst the better!'

Neal's gaze had been raking her and as she paused for breath he said tight-lipped, 'You weren't being very clever running off with this winsome seducer.'

'What's good enough for one adult in this party is good enough for another!' she flashed at him, her smile full of the hurt she was feeling inside.

'If you want to play husbands and wives,' said Neal, letting this shot glance off him, 'what's wrong with the little sailor boy? I thought you liked wandering hand in hand with him on the beach?'

'You mean that's what *you* like, to palm me off with Conrad because you know he'll never be anything to me but a friend.'

'And Stuart . . .?'

At the questioning intonation mingling with the sneer in Neal's voice Laraine choked, 'Don't be idiotic!'

This spurred Stuart to intervene. 'I've noticed you're pretty obsessed lately with your next-door company at Medway,' he said, his own lip curling, 'but I wasn't aware you'd also taken on the role of guardian for minor members of the family.'

'You forget I know your reputation,' Neal smiled grimly.

'But you obviously don't know *me*,' said Stuart, adding after a moment, 'would it put your mind at ease if I told you I haven't laid a finger on Laraine?'

'Not much,' Neal said flatly. 'You've been known to lie charmingly where women are concerned. But if I ever find out that you have I'll break your head, is that clear?'

Stuart's face took on a grey pallor. 'I think I'd better leave——'

'Do that. And look for someone else to do your flying too.'

'That won't be difficult. At least I'll get more than half-hearted co-operation for my money!'

'*Neal!*' Laraine's face was aghast. 'How can you talk to your friend like that? Stuart,' she turned appealingly, 'please don't go!'

'Let him be,' Neal snapped. 'And don't let me hear of you consenting to any more hare-brained schemes devised by our dissolute film star pal here.'

'As a matter of fact it was a lovely trip. I enjoyed it better than anything I've done since I came to the Bahamas,' Laraine lied with raised voice.

'That's only because you're kid enough not to know what you're getting yourself into.'

'Oh, always age!' she shouted tearfully. 'You never miss a chance to get that in, do you? Well, if you're an example of what it's like to be mature and experienced I'm glad I'm young and ignorant!'

As Stuart slammed out of the house she too flung herself away from the heated discussion. It only occurred to her as she was rushing blindly up the stairs to her room that Adele hadn't said a word.

The next day was one of abysmal despair for Laraine. She had said a lot of things to Neal that she didn't mean, and though she had enjoyed getting back at him for the profound hurt he had caused her by going off with Adele, there was no real satisfaction now to be felt for her actions, only gloom; a deep heartfelt gloom that cast a shadow over everything.

It was a strange day in more ways than one. Laraine was upset too about the fight between Neal and Stuart which for some reason she seemed to be the cause of. But it was Adele who was the main contributor to the uneasy atmosphere that hung over Medway. She drifted mechanically around the house saying nothing, but making it perfectly obvious by her attitude that she was not pleased.

Or perhaps it was something she was battling with inside which made her toss aside a magazine impatiently after glancing at the first few pages and go out to flop down on a lounger where she would, after a few minutes, jerk up and start plucking somewhat distractedly at the tendrils of blossom along the veranda.

Laraine took herself off to the beach where a grey pall seemed to blot out the sun, and when she got back to Medway in the evening things were no better. With a face like a marble mask Adele presided over dinner. Usually she never stopped giving orders to Benjamin the butler as to how to serve the meal, but tonight she seemed barely aware of his presence, though Benjamin, his white jacket a little big on his old shoulders and over-long at those ebony wrists, waited at table with his customary dignity, acquired no doubt through long years of dealing with all types of people.

But Laraine was not so adept at pretending that all was as it should be. Every mouthful of food she took seemed to stick in her throat and the more she tried to appear at ease the tenser she became inside. She had learned to tolerate the harsh tongue and satirical comments of her sister-in-law at the meal table, but this was a mood she had never seen before and quite frankly it unnerved her.

It seemed an age before the dessert arrived and after a few mouthfuls Laraine felt that she could decently retire to her room.

It was too early for bed and she wouldn't have been able to sleep anyway. There was no shaking off the oppressive feel of the night. In the end she decided to take a bath and get into bed with a book. The tepid water relaxed her a little and, towelled dry, she was tying a favourite old cotton negligé at her waist when a sound in the bedroom adjoining for some reason made her nerves twang to attention. It was with no surprise that she scuffed out of the bathroom to find Adele standing just inside the closed door of her room.

As Laraine emerged from the steamy vapours her sister-in-law said in tones that belied the companionable smile on her lips, 'Just like a young bride going through the pre-nuptial motions of bathing and oiling. I've done it myself, I'll admit. It all helps to recapture a past mood, and who can blame you desiring to live again the night you spent with Stuart on Cat Cay?'

Aware that her slim young form was perfectly visible through the worn negligé, and colouring hotly at Adele's sensual suggestions, Laraine said stiltedly, 'I don't know what all the fuss is about, just because Stuart and I took a holiday.'

'Is that all it was, pet—a holiday? As a close relative by marriage and your legal guardian I have a right to know just what exactly took place that night in the beach cottage at Cat Cay.'

Laraine had a feeling this was something her sister-in-law had been wanting to ask all day, and suddenly she enjoyed a curious sense of power; a surge of something primitive and feline which would not let her give a straight reply. 'As I said before,' she commented airily, 'I enjoyed the trip more than anything I've done since coming to the Bahamas.'

'Why, you little slut!' The mask was off and Adele's eyes were twin pockets of green fire in her white face. 'Is this the thanks I get for taking you from the back streets and giving you a decent home?'

'We had a reasonable place to live and a manageable income before you came along.' Laraine lifted her chin. 'You may have bought Richard, but you didn't buy me.'

'Richard!' Adele scoffed in a tired voice. 'A charming young man who quickly developed into a bore. And don't make out it was I who interfered in your pathetically homespun little lives. That brother of yours never gave me any peace from the moment he set eyes on me, and you know it.'

'He was frantically in love with you. Was it his fault that he was young and unaccustomed to bottling up his emotions?' Laraine's bosom heaved. 'No husband could have been more devoted to a wife, and you repaid him by running around behind his back with the worst kind of male companions!'

'Listen who's talking!' Adele jeered. 'You haven't wasted much time yourself in cornering the market where adulterers are concerned. Stuart is no Boy Scout—as you probably know by now.'

But Laraine had found an opening to give vent to her feelings held so long in check, and she was in no mood to be sidetracked now. 'Richard was a young and ardent lover. He had no idea that in demonstrating his affection he was becoming an embarrassment to you,' she said with tears in her eyes. 'His idea of marriage was a bond for life. He wanted you for always, not for just a few weeks of your time until the magic of his company wore off.'

'Richard got plenty out of me.' Adele waved a hand. 'I made up for my neglect of him, as you like to call it, by signing all the cheques for his expensive toys.'

'A machine capable of doing two hundred miles an hour is not a toy,' Laraine retorted. 'Or if it is, in the hands of an emotionally unstable young husband it's a lethal one.'

'What Richard did with the money I gave him was his own business,' Adele shrugged. 'I didn't mind keeping up the tag of wife just to suit him, but I'd no intention of acting as nursemaid to him because of his penchant for risking his neck.'

'You know that everything he ever did in the racing business he did for you,' Laraine said shakily.

'Yes, and isn't it ironic,' Adele's lips quirked coldly, 'that his final performance—careering into a concrete barrier on a wet and deserted track—gained no laurels at all—at least, only those in wreath form on his own grave.'

Laraine swallowed hard on the tears that were proving difficult to control. Angry and disgusted at this callous reply, she said quietly, 'I wouldn't have thought it possible that any woman could be so devoid of compassion or feeling for others.'

'Touché, my dear.' Adele's putty-coloured features tensed significantly. 'You should know. I'm willing to overlook the fact that you've made the most of your stay here in the Bahamas—which incidentally, I'm paying for—by indulging in whatever entertainment is going, including getting prettily under the feet of all my male visitors. But I wasn't aware that I'd given you the go-ahead to regard Stuart as your own personal property.'

'You may be paying for this trip,' Laraine flashed, 'but don't forget that I've been working for you as secretary and companion for two years and so I haven't seen a penny in wages. And my main reason for coming here was on your suggestion, to get away from everything that reminded me of Richard, not with any idea of basking in the millionaire playground kind of amusements and male adoration which appear to be so necessary to you.'

'On this holiday I've barely given a thought to the type of parties you detest,' Adele replied. 'And male adoration would have a far better chance of building into something interesting if you weren't always around putting on your poor little sister act. You must have played on Stuart's sympathies in a most appealing way.'

Stuart! Stuart! Stuart! Laraine was sick of the discussion. It hadn't done her any good airing her hurt about Richard. But she might have known it wouldn't. He belonged to a life that Adele had long since put behind her. Now she had other things on her mind; namely what had taken place during Laraine's stay on Cat Cay with a man whose reputation with women was well known. And exasperated to find that the implication of that leading question still lingered despite its being bogged down by senseless bickering, or rather because her sister-in-law chose to see that it did, she answered crossly at last. 'If you must know, Stuart took a sleeping bag outdoors on our overnight stay at Cat Cay. I locked myself in the beach cottage—not that there was any need—and never saw him again until he'd finished a round of golf at lunch-time the next day.'

Adele visibly slumped beside the door. She was still as pale as ever, though a small absent smile played about her lips as if she had heard something which had eased a crippling tautness within her. Then a miraculous change came over her. She had straightened when Laraine looked again; become almost regal with the new light in her eyes that was both secretive and yet in some strange way revealing. But the biggest surprise of all for Laraine was in hearing herself addressed by a voice that for once was neither patronising or satirical.

'I'm sorry our little talk developed into a slanging match,' Adele said, putting a hand out towards the door knob. 'I do have a certain responsibility towards you, you know, but it was not my intention to upset you with words that we both know are best left unsaid. Of course I'm glad to discover that you're still the little sister whom Richard adored, and I don't think I can be blamed for seeking, above all, to establish this. Goodnight, Laraine. I hope our silly little wrangle will in no way prevent you from having pleasant dreams.'

The door closed, but Laraine didn't remove her gaze from it until long after the slipper-clad footsteps had receded and faded out along the hall. *Adele showing the glimmerings of humility*. Was that possible? But hadn't there been something odd about her from the moment she had stepped into the room?

At the outset of the row Laraine had been ready to believe that her sister-in-law was like any other woman in that she would fight tooth and nail to defend her way of life. But tonight Adele's words had lacked fire, much of their usual bite. She had been like someone impatient with the ordinary victuals of an argument and eager to get to the peaches and cream; the sweet in this case being the discovery that Laraine had slept locked up tight on her own in the Cat Cay beach cottage.

Yes, Adele had certainly gone away doing her best to hide the dulcet smile on her lips.

It was this image of her sister-in-law floating erect and revitalised out of the room which gave Laraine much food for thought that night. As she lay in bed listening to the breeze-stirred murmurings of the sea and the rustling of beach palms it was not difficult to cast her mind back to a similar nocturnal scene. Stuart had talked a lot about his old flame June Shor that night outside the beach cottage on Cat Cay. It needed no special brain power to divine that she had been the romance of his life. Though he had accepted now that June no longer loved him he could not separate himself from the man he had once been in her eyes.

Laraine turned over and stared into the darkness. Content to live in the past, as far as the heart was concerned Stuart needed and wanted no one. But what about Adele? *What about Adele?*

The rear gardens seen through the vast lower pillars of Medway were at their loveliest. Faithfully watered by diligent workmen who came at dawn and disappeared before the house stirred, the green lawns were surpassed only by the trailing leafiness of the trees, and buttons of blossom in every shade bowed low as though in deference to the delicate beauty of border roses and flaming bird of paradise.

In contrast the inanimate and historical treasures of the house had to rely on the nostalgia they evoked from the past. Laraine stopped beside a brass-knobbed boot-rake, which was reputed to have been fashioned out of a Civil War cannon, without really seeing it. All she knew was that it made a handy place to prop herself against while she changed from house shoes to her comfortable old beach sandals which she usually discarded about here.

She had tidied the bedrooms, caught up with the business correspondence and arranged the meals for the rest of the day. Now with some spare time on her hands she knew what she meant to do.

Her fingers were not too steady and she was still fumbling with the buckle of one sandal when a figure appeared at the ground floor doorway and drifted across the pillar-enclosed terrace.

'Where are you off to?' Adele asked lightly, as though she had asked the question simply for something to do.

'I thought I'd go over and see Woodes,' Laraine said casually. 'He likes a romp, you know, and I'm supposed to exercise him every day.' This was not entirely true and she was careful to keep her head bent over her sandal. She missed the dog, but nowhere near as much as she missed Neal. It was like living in a grey bubble that would not let in light or laughter. She had never known such bleak discontent. She missed Neal's teasing tenderness, his tough sincerity, and she was ready to grasp at any excuse to see him again.

It was some days now since he had put in an appearance at Medway, not since the night of that awful row with Stuart, and with both men missing from the scene the house had never been quieter.

The buckle secured at last, she rose and was drifting off when Adele said behind her, 'Talking of exercise, I could do with some myself. I think I'll come with you for the walk.'

Too taken back to hide her surprise, Laraine turned and eyed her sister-in-law's slender-heeled shoes and frothy house dress. 'I'm going the beach way,' she said pointedly.

'I know,' Adele replied carelessly as though she was in the habit of tripping down the rough path to the sea-shore clad thus. Already carefully picking her way over the lawn, she said with a quick laugh, 'I'll manage.'

Laraine's heart sank. She had had visions of getting close to Neal, if not in the way she would have liked then at least through Woodes. Now it seemed that Adele had ideas of amusing herself with their next-door neighbour to while away the time.

They went down the flower-strewn incline that brought them to the beach, and here Laraine was met by another surprise. The stately yellow weeds, that waving sea of green and gold beyond the gate of Neal's property, had been razed to the ground and in its place were men and machinery and upturned soil.

Inside the gate she had no trouble pioneering a route in her simple footwear. Adele was game even though her pastel-stranded shoes disappeared altogether at times in the churned-up earth, which Laraine feeling more dejected than ever. Grit had never been one of her sister-in-law's strong points, but she seemed delicately determined to make this journey today.

Eventually they came upon Neal. Wearing only rough working shorts, his hard physique had been burnt dark by the sun. He saw them approaching and moved away from the commotion of field clearing to greet them—if one could call it that, Laraine thought wryly. He gave her a searing look, a flame-lit scrutiny which despite her intention to appear composed unsteadied her somewhat, then turned his attention to Adele.

'What are you doing, roughing it around here?' he asked with lazy concern. 'You could crick an ankle or something trying to negotiate these furrows in those shoes.'

'I'll admit this isn't my idea of having a pleasant stroll.' Adele accepted his steadying hand gratefully.

'Why have you done away with all the flowers?' Laraine asked in an accusing way, and, it was no use denying, to get into the picture.

'This land's lain idle long enough,' Neal shrugged. 'It's time something was done with it.'

'But it was so pretty before, now it's ruined!' Laraine looked around her in disgust.

'Trust a woman to go for ornamental values rather than practical ones,' Neal drawled. There was no green glow around them now to reflect the warmth in his eyes; just a dun-coloured flatness which about summed up his look after the initial impact of their meeting when his glance had raked hers. He kicked the dusty earth with his shoe and nodded at the barren stretches. 'I'm thinking of experimenting with sea-island cotton. This is one of the few estates where the topsoil is still good. And I owe it to the family name, I guess, to do something with the place.'

'Is that why we haven't seen you at Medway lately?' Adele queried, a quizzical slant to her smile.

'A man can't sit around and watch his possessions erode.' Neal's grin was tight. 'Sorry, Adele, but I've been wanting to put this scheme of mine into practice, and now at last the thing's under way.'

Laraine had a feeling that he was playing down his sudden enthusiasm for farming. By the sunburnt look of him he had spent his entire time since the night of that blazing row at Medway, out in the open, supervising the working of his land.

Adele pouted prettily. 'It would have to be the very time when I decide to pay a call. You're not very accommodating to your neighbours, are you, Neal?'

'You're not exactly the brogues and walking stick type. I didn't think it mattered if I ploughed up the field,' Neal retorted, not without humour. 'Why didn't you come by road as you always do?'

This was something which Laraine had been trying to puzzle out. It would not have been out of character for Adele to have ordered the car and demanded to be driven over to Neal's, despite the fact that it would have been encroaching on Laraine's free time. Her sister-in-law was accustomed to having her every whim obeyed, and she would certainly have arrived at Neal's looking her usual glamorous self. But this afternoon she had opted to accompany Laraine by way of the rustic route which even under normal conditions she must have known would be trying. Why?

Adele gave no clue by her smile. 'We wouldn't have found you in, obviously,' she said lightly. 'And I suppose now you're going to have us for trespassing, seeing that you've taken to cultivation on a grand scale.'

Adele never had any trouble in looking provocative, and

Neal was a man, after all. 'Of course not,' he gleamed. 'You've got this far, so you might as well come up to the house for a drink—only not the way you've been doing up to now. Here, let me give you a hand.'

He swung her up into his arms as though she weighed no more than one of the sheaves of pretty weeds stacked around, and Laraine followed one step behind. Seeing them together like this rekindled in her mind the pictures of the two of them on their paradise isle somewhere, and she wondered miserably why she had been foolish enough to tell Adele that she was thinking of calling in at Neal's—or for that matter why she had wanted to see him herself.

CHAPTER NINE

As they neared the rear garden area of the house colourful birds plumed out of a strip of greenery, one of the last to go under the steel jaws of an oncoming tractor. Having seen nothing but the usual seabirds so far on the island, Laraine felt a flash of pleasure at the jewelled flight, but that was all. There were other things to view which were not nearly as delighting to the eye.

Inside the gate Woodes was all over her. He fussed and yelped and jumped almost to her shoulder, and a least this gave her something to do during those first few strained moments of arrival. Neal set Adele down on firm ground near the house, where she took one shocked look at herself and exclaimed, 'Heavens, aren't I a sight! Is there anywhere I can clean up?'

'First door along the right inside.' Neal nodded towards the interior.

Left alone with him, Laraine felt awkward and unhappy. She was dusty herself, but in her old beach attire it hardly seemed to matter. However, she couldn't just stand around now that Woodes had deserted her in favour of a juicy bone, tossed recently, it seemed, from the kitchen window, so she went to the well. She could just as easily sluice down here as anywhere.

It would have been no trouble to draw up the water and she resented Neal's assistance in the task. It made her feel worse because it reminded her of another time when they had propped themselves together near the old well like this. A time when, though she had fought with him on that very first occasion over the fate of Woodes, the sky above them had never been bluer and the emerald glow of the flowering meadow had given a charitable depth to his eyes. Now all that was gone. Outside was a dun-coloured world and there was a distance between them which had never been there on their most heated of disagreements.

In sun-bleached shorts and brief top, an old straw hat clamped on her head, they might have been transported back in time. Only Neal was different. She hadn't asked him to tug up the bucket, but he had done so anyway and, tight-lipped, he took control of the brimming contents while she hung on to the rope with stubborn independence.

'Stand aside while I set it down,' he growled, 'or we're both going to get soaked.' Laraine had no choice but to watch him swing the bucket out with an effortless jerk of his wrist and as it slopped down on the step beside her she said ungraciously, 'You needn't have bothered. I'm perfectly capable of drawing my own washing water.'

'This place is becoming too handy a spot for ablutions,' he said, dipping into the water himself. 'To say nothing of it being decidedly indecorous. I'm thinking of dispensing with the well anyway. It's outgrown its usefulness in an age of tapped water and irrigation jets.'

Laraine was aghast at the thought. To remove the ornamental stonework of the well would be to demolish most of the charm of this tucked-away garden. But she couldn't bring herself to argue in the old intimate way with Neal. Instead she eased the most recent hurt by commenting between splashes, 'If you do that the men of the house won't be able to display their virile capabilities—although I'll admit there are other ways.'

He seemed amused in an unsmiling fashion that the transportation of Adele in his arms had irked her. 'Don't tell me those kittenish ways are showing signs of she-cat tendencies,' he said, drying himself off on a clean rag he had found.

Laraine reached to share the cloth with him. She wasn't thinking of the well now but of the seductiveness of her sister-in-law. 'Talking of ornamental values,' she smiled obtusely, 'you called me a woman back there in the meadow. Just a slip of the tongue, I suppose?'

'Not at all,' his gaze had sparked up again. 'After your night on Cat Cay with Meller I don't see that we can regard you as anything else.'

'You're not still harping on *that*!' she sparked back at him, making no secret of her exasperation.

'Why not?' he shrugged with sour humour. 'I thought you'd be dying to discuss the subject. Doesn't every woman want to talk about her conquests, especially the first one?'

'And what about the men?' she flashed. 'Or would that mean a non-stop commentary running into enough words to fill a book?'

'In the old days,' he countered with a grim smile, 'we used to tell our children, "Do as I say, not as I do".'

'That's all right for children,' she retorted pointedly. 'And anyway, who said anything about first conquests? How do you know I haven't had a string of boy-friends?'

'I know.' He wore a look of male shrewdness that irritated her. 'When I first met you, you were one step from the schoolroom.'

'You can't stop progress,' she said loftily.

'Progress is all right.' He let his gaze saunter over her youthful figure, with its notable curves in brief beachwear. 'What you haven't got to do is try to go too fast.'

For some reason his superior, know-it-all manner inflamed her. 'I'll move as fast as I like, *Mister* Hansen!' she threw the cloth at him with force. 'I emerged from my childhood cocoon ages ago, and I don't intend to wear it round my neck as a memento just because it suits *you* to keep it there!'

He blinked at this outburst as though her words had touched on an unknown nerve within him. But this unexpected undercut did not dilute an old anger in him and between his teeth he replied, 'There are times when I could——'

'What?' she confronted him unflinchingly. 'Teach me a lesson like you did once before when I flaunted your vast authority on the subject of romance? If anyone brought me a long way from the schoolroom, it was you!'

'You asked for it,' he glinted. 'And maybe Meller was faced with the same dilemma.'

'Well, that's something you'll never know, isn't it?' she crowed quiveringly.

'You little mopsy! I ought to put you over my——'

'Now, children, no fighting please!' Adele had reappeared and she spoke with a kind of benign maturity as though she didn't mind at all assuming the role of the wise elder. 'We don't want a recurrence of the other night, do we?' she said, arranging the skirt folds of her dress. 'And by the way, Neal, I've just thought of something. Why don't you give Stuart a ring and make it up to him? It's silly for two grown-up men to sulk because of a little argument.'

'Excuse me, I have to go in and find a shirt,' said Neal with clamped jaw. 'I'll be along to pour your drinks in a moment.' He waited for the two of them to precede him indoors, then disappeared.

Laraine led the way into the long room that was the lounge, wondering if Adele really had just thought of contacting Stuart. But only fleetingly. She was feeling too wretched to care. She hadn't meant to quarrel like that with Neal. All her plans to get back on the old footing with him seemed to have gone awry. So much so that the chances of recapturing the comradely atmosphere of those days when they had argued cheerfully over Woodes and splashed as a laughing threesome along the beach were more miserably remote than ever.

Adele arranged herself on the long wallside sofa. Laraine chose a chair beside the inner doorway so that when Neal walked in, the sight of him in cream knitted shirt and slacks, all coppery from his field days in the sun, made her want to cry out with love for him.

It was a cry that would have fallen flat on its face. He was like new leather that hasn't learnt to give with use. She could almost hear the creak of his antagonism as he passed her chair for the drinks cabinet.

His duty done as a host, he went to sit beside Adele, but for once she appeared to have little interest in the contents of her glass. She had certainly done a good job of removing the dust from her person and looked delicately appealing in her pleated nylon dress patterned with tiny lilac flowers. 'Please, Neal,' she brushed close to him, 'won't you do it for me? We feel awful about what happened that night at Medway. You and Stuart were such good friends. Men shouldn't let the trivialities of us females come between them. I for one won't rest until the two of you have made it up.'

'Try your drink,' Neal said tersely. 'I'll think about it.'

Adele did as she was told, but her fluttering glance kept straying his way and after a while he rose unhurriedly and moved towards the phone. The number he dialled must have proved negative, for away from the earpiece he said, 'He's not at his hotel.'

'Try the Reef Club,' said Adele, watching him.

After a few moments Neal got through. There was another lapse and then he could be heard tightly greeting Stuart.

Adele's look of tense expectation died down to one of secret relief. Laraine had been eyeing her sister-in-law curiously, and suddenly with that look so much slotted into place. She knew now that Adele bickered incessantly with Stuart because unlike any other man she had met before he did something to her. Effortlessly—and ironically, unlike other men, without trying—he had penetrated that sacred domain of hers, her inner self. And always the one to call the tune where men were concerned, she had battled with all she possessed to prevent it.

Even when Stuart had twinklingly suggested that Adele accompany him to Cat Cay she had rejected him with what strength she could muster and elected to go away with Neal instead. But the day after Laraine's own return from Cat Cay with Stuart had been a bad one for Adele. From morning till evening she had fought a losing battle with her feelings and in the end she had had to have it out with Laraine. And an hour ago, when she had learned that Laraine was coming over to Neal's place, afraid that if she waited for the car she would succeed in talking herself out of it, she had struck out along the rough route in spindly-heeled shoes. Now she was here and she was asking, albeit indirectly, to see Stuart.

Because of her tumbling thoughts Laraine was aware only vaguely of the brief exchanges over the phone conducted, it seemed, in a civil manner. The next thing she knew Neal was replacing the receiver and saying to the room, 'He's coming over.'

Adele seemed satisfied and in no way put out at the thought of a wait. For her part Laraine didn't know how she was going to get through the awkwardness of the interlude with the three of them twiddling their thumbs in Neal's lounge. He hadn't looked her way since entering the room and he had made it perfectly clear by the rigid set of his shoulders that he was prepared to repair his friendship with Stuart for Adele's sake, not for hers.

As it happened Stuart was not too long in making the

journey from the Coral Reef Country Club; although his advent into the Hansen household couldn't have been called anything but strained. The first thing he did when he entered the room was to stick out his hand to grip Neal's. 'I've missed you, you old son of a gun,' he said, not without feeling.

Neal clapped him round the shoulder. 'Next time you go flirting with a filly just out of the paddock make sure it's not too close to home.' He dismissed the subject of the tiff with a bent grin. 'Now what will you have to drink?'

While it was being poured the men chatted idly about what they had been doing during the past few days. Though Neal couldn't have been more hospitable Laraine sensed that there was some small part of him that was withdrawn, that there would always be this invisible barrier now between the two friends, and she felt sad then that the ways of men and women could create such havoc among themselves.

She was also bristling inwardly at Neal's offhand 'filly' remark, as though this summed up her presence in the room and at the same time dispensed with it. Obviously she was not expected to have any say in the general amnesty that was taking place.

Not that Adele's opening lines were any more friendly than those she had made in the past. Though it was clear now why she had worked so hard to remove all traces of the dusky trek, for reclining at this moment, slender legs crossed, no woman could have looked more inviting. Dark lashes swooping low, she drawled, 'We gathered our company compares poorly with that wench of a boat of yours, but I wouldn't have believed you'd forgo the pleasures of free whisky and subtle chat for a whole week!'

'Did you miss me, darling?' Stuart gave her his thick-skinned smile.

'Like the toothache,' she replied.

'It's sometimes nice to have pain—the kind you can

explore to the point of almost enjoying it.' There was a dark ambience in his eyes which seemed to ignite something in Adele's hooded green glance, but she answered in her usual corrosive vein.

'If that's supposed to describe your turning up again, enjoyment is not the word I would have used.'

'Well, I keep working at it,' he sighed cheerfully.

Their sparring was like old times, then Stuart broke off to glance across the room and, irrepressible as ever, he spoke up. 'Hi, Laraine! How've you been?'

She sat on the edge of her straight-backed chair, aware of Neal's eyes flaming her way, and of another jade gaze fixed on her. And though she had told herself adamantly at the start that she had every right to join in the reconciliation with Stuart, she was suddenly stuck for words.

It was Adele who bridged the uncomfortable pause. 'Come on, Larry,' she joked purringly, 'say hello to the nice gentleman.'

Neal had strolled over and taking the glass of the foul stuff he had poured for her from her hand he said with a malicious gleam, 'Your drink needs topping up.'

Knowing that he had given her the hardest liquor he could find in so-called recognition of her bridging the gap between adolescence and womanhood was all Laraine needed to recover her voice, and with an impish smile that matched that of the other man she reciprocated lightly, 'Hi, Stuart, I'm fine, how are you?'

'Great now that we're all together again,' he said sincerely. And after a while, when the general atmosphere of the room did appear to be lighthearted, he suggested out of the blue, 'Hey, why don't we all take off in the *Melanie* and go picknicking and deck-lazing like old times?'

'I've got a better idea,' Adele put in from her place on the spacious sofa.

'Okay, let's have it,' Stuart grinned.

'Not now.' She slid her glass down carefully on the coffee table. 'First of all I want you both to promise that you'll come to Medway tomorrow night for dinner. Will you do that?'

While the two male members of the group were looking at each other and shrugging their assent she added with a little laugh, 'I'll settle for nothing less than bow ties and dinner jackets, remember. This is to be a very special occasion. Larry and I want to make up for the upset of the past week, don't we, Larry, and what better way than to put on something of a ball for the four of us?'

Sparkling parties presented no problem when there was money to burn. But what was the reason for suggesting it? Adele was acting mysterious again and Laraine didn't like it. However, she knew there was no point in showing surprise at her sister-in-law's remarks, for as in the past, on occasions like this, her agreement was taken for granted.

'And what about this idea of yours?' Stuart asked, an intrigued look mingling with his usual mocking expression.

'I'll tell you about that,' Adele replied tantalisingly, 'when we see you tomorrow night.'

To clinch the date they all had another drink of which Laraine valiantly took several swigs of hers. Then Stuart dropped the two girls off at Medway on his way back to town, a journey which Laraine had little recollection of, as her head floated giddily on her shoulders in a most uncontrolled fashion.

The next day was a busy one, with Adele issuing orders for this and that to be done, so that there was little time to wonder what was going on behind those over-bright green eyes of hers. She wanted her favourite hairdresser up from Nassau, and extra staff to be engaged to supplement the services of Benjamin and his help in the kitchen. Also at her request one of the unused rooms was opened up and dusted for the occasion.

Towards evening when much of the bustle had died down and a peculiar air of expectation hung over the house, Laraine was up in her room wondering half-heartedly what she should wear for Adele's party. A visit from her sister-in-law was the last thing she expected at the moment, and when the door opened and the satin-house-coated figure slid in she thought it must be because of some last-minute request she had forgotten to attend to.

Adele, however, seemed more concerned now with the personal kind of preparation. 'Here put this on tonight,' she tossed a froth of white tulle and silver on the bed. 'I've been looking through my things and I think this will fit you all right.'

Having spent all afternoon under the skilful hands of the hairdresser Adele was not, it seemed, inclined to give away any secrets, for the finished results were hidden under a large chiffon square. But Laraine's gaze was directed towards the bed. She picked up the dress in awe and exclaimed, 'It's beautiful! I couldn't!'

'Wear it. You'll look sweet in it.' It was an order softened, for once, by an enigmatic smile. 'And haven't I said that tonight is to be a special occasion?'

If Adele said it was to be so, then so it would be, and as she left the room Laraine fingered the dress, both dubious and captivated.

Later when she had used a lavender soap and matching cologne secreted away for special occasions she slipped into the ice-white dress, a little worried to find that her youthful contours were rather more robust than Adele's willowy slenderness so that the tight white bodice outlined quite noticably the small curve of her breasts. And the silver straps were inclined, if she didn't keep her attention on them, to slip off her shoulders. But it was an expensive dress and there was no denying that she looked attractive in it.

Of course her hair-style was a little too simple for so sophisticated a creation, and her shoes were a bit of a let-down, pale casuals against the shin-length gossamer skirt. But on the plus side the honey-gold tan that she had acquired so carelessly while drifting about out of doors diverted the eye from most of the flaws in her appearance.

And anyway, she told herself with a sudden flatness after all her efforts, it was only Adele's party.

Downstairs she had to bypass several rooms to arrive at the one that Adele had chosen for the evening. The decor consisted mainly of ivory paintwork and black-bordered prints on the walls. The twin staircases flanking the huge fireplace area, which was also painted white, were of a rich dark wood and were said to resemble a deer's antlers. Two black and white porcelain ducks graced the mantelpiece beside a black and gold clock of antique design, and but for the Aubusson carpet centred between the staircases and giving length to the floor space, the room had an almost clinical neatness.

It was an odd one to choose for a party; even the bowl of flowers on the crystal and silver-decked table were in ice-white. But as Laraine was soon to discover, Adele knew what she was doing in selecting it for the occasion.

The cars arrived and the two men came in together, shown through by the slow-moving Benjamin. Though Laraine was achingly conscious of Neal, looking spruce in evening dress, her gaze went straight to the rakishly handsome figure of Stuart, who took her hands between his and remarked appraisingly, 'You look like my favourite ice-cream topped by silver cachous—is it permitted to sample the flavour?'

'Of course,' she laughed as he kissed her cheek with mouthwatering playfulness. 'I can assure you I won't melt.'

With a fixed smile she acknowledged Neal's greeting, blazingly aware, that, in contrast to Stuart's open admiration of her appearance, his keen and contemptuous gaze was noting the floppy shoulder straps of her dress, and its badly-fitting bodice. And her make-up, which up to then she considered she had applied rather skilfully, now felt like a mud-pack on her face.

It was a shortlived look, fortunately, for on the heels of the men Adele was making her grand entrance. Knowing how long she had spent getting ready for this moment Laraine was prepared for something spectacular, but nothing she could have imagined would have done justice to the picture her sister-in-law made tonight.

Her reed-like slenderness was encased in a sheath dress of metallic silk shot with emerald lights. A satin V-shaped vent starting centrally at the thighs and widening into a froth of green fire gave a seductive curve to her hips and matched the banked-down excitement in her eyes. Her alabaster shoulders were bare, devoid of all decoration except a fine gold chain on which a heavy crystal droplet nestled in the smooth well of her breasts.

Exquisitely made up as always, a ringleted Empress Josephine hair-style gave her a dignity and grace which her dress, for all its daring design, could not dispel.

The men of course were bowled over. Neal embraced her to show his appreciation, a gesture which sent a fresh stab of misery through Laraine. Of course, she recalled, the two of them had been away together, so what could be more natural than a familiar embrace?

Stuart viewed Adele with his old mocking charm and the light of puzzlement in his eyes as he kissed her hand in cavalier fashion. 'By all the saints!' he drawled, adhering faithfully to the role. 'If I'd known we were going to be entertained so royally I'd have put on my court sash and my medals.'

'Come and sit down, Stuart, and stop your fool games,' Adele said tolerantly, taking his hand.

She was a little nervous tonight, though this was not apparent in her smooth handling of seating arrangements at the table. And one could see now why she had chosen this particular room in which to dine. In the cool and austere setting she sparkled like a warm and lovely gem on a colourless background. Clever Adele!

The meal was faultless, as Adele had intended it would be, though much of the work in organising its perfection had fallen on Laraine's shoulders. Bahamian dishes giving off exotic aromas were wheeled in on a silver trolley, followed by coconut salad and fruits carved in the shape of flowers.

The talk at the table was general as though this sort of thing went on all the time, though everyone knew that there was a purpose behind tonight's get-together and besides an air of expectancy an amused kind of tension hung over the meal.

Laraine for one had not felt at ease since she had taken her place opposite Neal at the table. Never once during the evening had she been able to forget the dreadful flaws in her appearance, which in all probability were noticeable to only her and Neal. She was convinced that Adele, apart from making sure that the dress she offered would not overshadow her own attire, had genuinely wanted her to look her best tonight, and unwittingly—not knowing about the drooping shoulder-straps and barely breathable bodice—she had enhanced her own meticulous experience and flawless beauty by the very contrast. Once again, of course, solely where Neal's gaze was concerned.

However, Laraine was able to ignore most of his secret disparagement by listening to the talk at the table and obeying Adele's numerous requests to be passed this and that during the meal. 'Larry, be a pet and reach me the conch sauce. I do think it brings out the flavour of these turtle cutlets.' Or 'Larry, honey, why don't we try a dash of rum-raisin essence with our tropical fruit—I think I can see it beside the salad bowl.'

Naturally with Stuart and Adele seated at such close range it wasn't only the sauces that were piquant. Their verbal exchanges made the most biting of flavours appear bland, and towards the coffee stage when Laraine had been directed to pass the dish of molasses from Neal's side of the table, which was 'so much better' than brown sugar with coffee, Stuart asked, 'Why do you always treat Laraine like a kid sister instead of a responsible individual? Is it because this way she makes a handy skivvy for your petty requirements?'

'Do I?' Adele's innocent green eyes flew wide. 'Always treat Laraine like a kid sister?' She pondered on this and said, 'I suppose I've always regarded her as an infant to be guided, but I can see your point. She's looking anything but that tonight.'

'I second that statement.' Stuart raised his wine glass. 'She's as pretty as a picture—a womanly one, not a babe. But this isn't something that's happened overnight. It's been stealing up on us in a most delightful way——'

'Since about a week ago,' Adele put in smoothly but pointedly. 'Who are we to argue when you yourself have been instrumental in provoking this striking metamorphosis?'

No mention was made of Cat Cay, but Stuart replied with his mocking charm, 'I do my best to bring out the stars in the ladies' eyes.'

It was a typical rakish comment, delivered no doubt with a view to expansion, but for once Adele didn't rise to the bait. Her fingers were trembling slightly on her coffee cup. She said after a moment, 'Anyway, we're all agreed that Laraine is no longer a child. That puts her on an equal footing with the rest of us—makes her one of the clan, right?' Without waiting for any overall response she added, lowering her cup with feline grace, 'And that brings me to this idea of mine.'

Since the previous afternoon Adele's behaviour had been nothing short of mysterious and they all felt involved. Neal, sitting at the other side of the resplendent table with the ease acquired no doubt from his airline captain days, looked grimly intrigued. Stuart draped an arm over the back of his chair and drawled with his provocating grin, 'I thought you'd never get round to it.'

For a second Adele looked unsure of herself, then she began, 'For a week now our little group has not been what it used to be. We're all dissatisfied in some way or gone stale with the rules of the game. We've all been away and yet our togetherness isn't the thing it was. Well, we can go away again, only this time treading new ground, as it were. Nowadays there's a remedy for a foursome who want a break from routine.' She took a quick smiling breath and concluded, 'They swop partners.'

Adele's slant on the situation was hazy and out of focus, but she had managed to convey the meaning she desired and Stuart leaned forward a little, his eyes playfully aglow as he spelled it out. 'You mean Neal takes off with Laraine somewhere and you and I team up for some spree?'

Adele didn't speak, but her expression told its own story. Seeing it, Laraine was aghast. Now she knew the reason for the pretty dress loaned for the occasion, and the constant requests for this and that item on the table, all, she realised now, situated around the area of a certain masculine presence. Adele had been quietly throwing her at Neal's head because she wanted Stuart.

Her and Neal! Oh, that would be screamingly funny if it wasn't so heartbreakingly awful. Adele didn't know that Neal was in love with his stewardess, the far distant Stephanie, and that his relationship with Adele had been for the purpose of playing tit-for-tat in some way, or perpetuating tormenting thoughts of Stephanie in his mind.

Oh yes, Adele had certainly set the scene for something tonight! But despite a feeling of annoyance and distaste Laraine couldn't be angry with her. Adele had organised the evening in a dazzling way—her alluring appearance was evidence of that—not as a woman out to ensnare, but as a woman who desperately needed to be wanted. She could deny this with her tongue, but not with her heart. And watching the way Stuart was viewing her with laconic appraisal there was, to Laraine's mind, something vaguely pathetic about it all.

Stuart was the first to put his seal on the idea. 'The arrangement suits me fine,' he said, his eyes on Adele's mouth from which had escaped a tiny gasp through smiling, parted lips.

Laraine didn't know where to put her own gaze. Without her wanting it to it jerked across the table where she saw Neal say with tight-lipped approval, 'I'm game.'

CHAPTER TEN

LARAINE couldn't believe her ears. What did Neal think he was trying to prove, making a reply like that? That she would go away with any man at the crook of a finger? Just because she had taken off with Stuart. Or that she wasn't 'grown up' enough to cope with the challenge? Either way she was having no part of a set-up contrived to fling her into Neal's arms. And after he had been away with Adele!

Her cheeks aflame, she blurted, 'Well, I think it's a crazy idea. Weird, in fact!'

'Three to one. You're outvoted, pet,' said Adele with a feverish happiness in her green eyes. 'The pact's been made and I don't think we should linger in putting it into practice.'

Stuart said, 'The *Melanie*'s all spruced up, and there's a trip I've been meaning to make to Crooked Island. I could pick you up at dawn.'

Adele nodded, not looking directly his way. 'I'll pack tonight.'

Laraine jumped up, not caring about the rattle of her coffee cup as she did so. 'Well, you can count me out,' she said in the most level tones she could muster. 'And if you'll excuse me, I think I'll go to my room now.'

Her cheeks were still painfully hot when a short while later she heard the cars departing down on the drive outside. She hadn't bothered to put on a light in her room and the glow of the headlights as the cars swung illuminated momentarily its vintage decor and proportions. She tried several times to fasten her thoughts on to something else, and wondered absently what it must have been like occupying such a room in the days when horse-drawn carriages had passed by beneath the window.

But her mind could not shake itself free of the bizarre happenings which had taken place downstairs. Only in a house where money flowed freely, only with a sister-in-law like Adele, who always managed to create an atmosphere a little larger than life, would such a situation have been possible.

She heard Adele come up to her room and close the door speedily behind her. For long enough Laraine stood with her own thoughts, then, unable to stay put any longer, she went out and along the upstairs hallway and knocked on the door of Adele's room.

She hadn't expected to get a reply, nor did the scene before her when she opened the door and entered come as much of a surprise.

Adele had changed into a flowing negligé and was tossing wispy garments into the suitcase lying open on the bed.

Laraine looked at her sister-in-law and said as the slim white hands worked feverishly at the task of filling the overnight case, 'He doesn't love you, Adele.'

'I know,' Adele gave a little broken laugh and worked brisker than ever at the business of packing. 'And wouldn't you think,' she folded a gossamer-skirted gown in a shaky way, 'that I, of all people, would welcome such a trouble-free arrangement?' Her eyes were brilliantly lit, filmed with something that was not all triumph and satisfaction. something that went straight to Laraine's heart.

Taking a step forward, she said, amazed at her own trembling tones, 'Don't go, Adele. If you know what you know don't go through with this silly pact.'

She might have been talking to a sleepwalker, a fervent-eyed somnambulist who moved in her own rosy world of makebelieve. The only words that Adele was sufficiently cognizant to impart as she shut and locked the case and made preparations for bed were the determined and damped-down excited ones, 'I'm going!'

Laraine, realising it was useless to argue since it would have been like battling with a feather in a breeze, returned to her own room and spent a restless night, only dropping off when the old Massachusetts chiming clock on the stairway had musically struck three.

She missed Adele's going, heard nothing of Stuart's car, and only knew of their departure when Benjamin asked where she would like to take her solitary breakfast. Eating alone was nothing new to Laraine, as her sister-in-law invariably breakfasted in bed. But the elderly manservant, twinkingly aware that she might like a break from routine, suggested the timber-framed card saloon with its views of tumbling flowered rockery and sun-refracted sea depths.

Laraine had to smile to herself. Benjamin, despite his ebony dignity, was a gentle soul and in sympathy, she suspected, with her position as underling to an autocractic sister-in-law. But she was not happy breakfasting in lone splendour even though the mellow woodwork and masculine bric-à-brac of the card saloon were soothing to the eye. Nor did she notice much of the dramatic views from the alcoved windows. There had been nothing autocratic about Adele last night. And every time Laraine thought about last night she wanted to pull a shutter down in her mind and lock and bar it for all time. Never to go back to those palpitating, never-ending moments at the dinner table when Neal's derogatory gaze had wandered over her appearance. Or to know again the sickening impact of his words, calmly delivered, when he had told Adele, 'I'm game' in reply to her crazy scheme. And she wouldn't *She wouldn't.* The shutter was down and there it would stay.

So as not to disappoint Benjamin too much after the trouble he had taken she demolished what she could of the contents of the breakfast dishes, then retired to her room.

But its antique sedateness and unreal atmosphere rankled in her present mood and she knew she would have to get out into the wild free air of the beach.

With Adele away and no duties to attend to she was free to roam where she pleased. But there would be no childish get-up of frayed shorts and carelessly knotted sun-top today. She had grown out of that phase of her life. It had happened that afternoon in Neal's garden when he had taken her roughly in his arms and kissed her with a savagery that had both shocked and pierced her with a radiant longing for something other than scorn from his lips, something sweeter than coarse ravishment from his touch.

A pair of figure-moulding slacks in bold and brilliant blue were much more in keeping with this new person she had become. And a white blouse with crisp stand-up collar and cap sleeves gave her a sophistication she was proud of. Proud, but not happy; she caught the reflection of her shadowed eyes and pale face in the mirror. Knowing oneself to be in love was the most golden of realisations, but in her own case there could never be any crowning fulfilment. She was bound by invisible ties, by all it was that made her live and breathe, to a man whose heart and mind, in turn, were on the other side of the world, fettered to a girl he had been unable to forget despite the seductive attentions of a woman as beautiful as Adele.

As she traversed the woodland steps, the sound of the sea murmuring through the gaps in the trees, it occurred to Laraine that her sling-back casuals would perhaps not be the ideal footwear for plodding through fine-grained sand. But she couldn't be bothered to go back and change. After the splurge of feminine assertion she had lost interest in her appearance and decided that if her shoes became a nuisance she could just as well take them off and go barefoot.

The fragrance of sea and sand and sun-soaked palms in her nostrils, the unbroken calm of the beach, lifted her feet sufficiently to make for firmer walking along the sea's edge, but not her heart. How was it possible to know that loveliness abounded and yet not feel or taste it in one's mind? The only thing she could feel and hurt over was her love for Neal, and that didn't improve her appreciation of the views one bit. The heels of her shoes were making sucking noises in the wet sand. She obviously wasn't going to get far like this. The sensible thing to do would be to go barefoot and slap along over the glistening damp. Thinking about it half-heartedly she was glad she didn't actually go through with the idea and forfeit her dignity, for while she was idly noticing the watery pockets her heels made behind she saw Neal drifting towards her.

Neal. The image and the man!

He seemed to appear from nowhere as though he hadn't been very far away from the start. With his coming the scenery seemed suddenly drenched in colour. Her surroundings were etched in the most superb clarity, lit, not by the sun, but by the central force of his presence.

He was wearing linen beach slacks and an unzipped lightweight flying jacket, and with the breeze flicking his hair into tousled copper-lit strands, he looked hardbitten and lovable. But the shutter had dislodged slightly and Laraine was remembering last night.

Strolling beside her, he looked her over as though what he saw came as no surprise. 'Taking a walk?' he asked.

'It would appear so, wouldn't it?' Her reply was icy.

'I fancy a spot of exercise myself,' he said with his tight smile. 'Why don't we take a stroll round my estate?'

'And see Woodes?' Her heart lifted slightly.

'Later, maybe.' Neal's gaze was somewhat hooded. 'I was thinking I'd show you the section I'm setting aside for growing pineapples.'

Laraine looked along the beach into the distance to where she had vaguely been planning to view the palm-screened residences on the way to town. It was in the opposite direction to Neal's place. She had chosen the route for that very reason. But now all her firm intentions were dwindling simply because Neal was indicating the way.

Through the wicker gate the ground had been levelled and the going was nowhere near as difficult as it had been last time, although Laraine's shoes still proved to be a nuisance and at one point when they were traversing the stretch flanking the back garden area of the house, Neal said testily, 'You look great in your out-of-the-schoolroom get-up, but do you have to punish your feet to prove a point?'

Laraine flashed him a look and refused his helping hand, remarking haughtily, 'I can manage, thank you.'

They skirted the house grounds some distance away and came upon a barren stretch along its south side, an open plot baked hard by the sun and the buffeting trade winds. But it wasn't the weed-stunted emptiness that caught Laraine's eye. She barely noticed it, for gleaming in the sunlight some distance away, like some tropical, enamelled dragonfly sunning its wings before darting off, was Neal's Cherokee sports plane.

He continued walking pointing across the space. 'Over there beyond the bordering tamarisks is where I'm planning to set up the pineapple plantation.' And then as though he must make some mention of the plane he said casually, 'This section near the house makes a handy air-strip. When the weather's good it's convenient to flip in and out from one's own grounds.'

Laraine didn't know, but she felt sure that Neal had always used the official air-strip on the island to house and run his plane. She certainly had never heard it or seen it in these parts before. But it was a line of thought that faded from her mind before she could think to pursue it. Naturally she was interested in the dashing little light aircraft, but more because it had housed Neal and Adele in the intimacy of its interior on their paradise island trip.

'Growing pineapples used to be one of the main occupations in the Bahamas. A group of German refugees introduced the idea and at one time the fruit used to be uprooted and stored aboard sailing vessels as complete plants. They were watered and looked after during the voyage so that diners in London restaurants could pick the fruit at their tables. It's not like that today, of course.' Neal seemed to be talking rather a lot. 'A long time ago Hawaii cornered the pineapple market. They built it into a streamlined industry and the Bahamas could no longer compete. But I've a feeling there's plenty of business to be got with local restaurants and hotels and it's on the cards I'll sell all I grow.'

He led her across a route that came within a couple of yards of the poised red dragonfly. Laraine must have been craning her neck without realising it, for Neal said lazily as they were passing the plane, 'You can take a closer look if you like.'

The temptation to torment herself with visions of Adele sitting cosily in the seat next to the pilot's was powerful in Laraine. And with a kind of masochistic fascination she moved in closer to view the padded and no doubt perfume-impregnated, she told herself dispiritedly, interior.

All at once Neal swept her up in his arms. Mystified and surprised, the only thing Laraine could suppose in those first few moments was that he had at last grown tired of her hobbled way of walking and decided to transport her the last few yards to the pineapple patch in this fashion to save time. *But he wasn't going that way*. By the time she realised that she was going to get more than a ground's-eye view of the interior of the plane Neal had dumped her inside swung in himself and they were taxiing over the weed-stunted field towards the sea.

It had all happened so fast Laraine was still trying to unravel herself from her seat when they were soaring over translucent sand and coral-patterned waters, and heading for the sun.

It didn't take her long to arrive at the conclusion that she had been duped in some way, and to be got the better of by someone like Neal made her tearfully furious.

'Just what to you think you're doing?' She all but threw herself at him. 'Take me back this minute!'

'Uh-uh,' he shook his head with maddening complacency. 'You don't back out of a game that's only half over. That's cheating.'

'I'm not the participant in any game!' She stumbled over her pedantic choice of words, then recovered herself to flash, knowing full well what he was referring to. '*I* don't have to amuse myself with such childish pastimes!'

'You're the one who started it,' he smiled, clicking her seat belt into place with grim finality. 'And you don't start something unless you finish it. At least not in my book, you don't.'

His menacing attitude unnerved Laraine, but she had no intention of letting him see it. She threw an exasperated glance to the roof of her flying prison and writhed, 'If you're talking about this . . . this swapping partners lunacy, *I've* had no hand in it. *You* went away with Adele in the first place, remember?'

'But you started the ball rolling by pairing off with Stuart, now the thing has to run its course.'

She glowered at the typical male way of twisting things to put the fault elsewhere and flung back at him, 'Why? Because it suits Adele to invent these crazy situations?'

'No.' Neal flicked the joystick, making their eager winged mount leap forward. 'Because *I* say when you start something you finish it.'

She was sobered sufficiently to drop back in the seat. But her mind was going over the meek way she had walked into the trap and flouncing again she jeered with disgust, 'Pineapple plantation! I bet you're not thinking of any such scheme.'

'Scout's honour,' he grinned in a way that made her love him and hate him at the same time, 'It's a plan I've had in mind for some time.'

Laraine condescended to look out of the window. They were flying quite close to the water now. Limpid, having no colour of its own, it took its hues from the depth and character of the ocean floor. Purple-brown shades threaded with the yellow gleam of sea-fans indicated live coral. Dark green areas would be patches of sea-grass. There were lanes of clear blue and mounds of pure white where shoals of sand almost reached the surface in places.

After a while Laraine asked moodily, 'Where are we going?'

'To a tucked-away place that not many people know about,' Neal said comfortably.

Laraine gripped the arms of her seat. *He was taking her to the paradise island where he had stayed with Adele.* She couldn't bear it! It might be all one big joke to Neal. But it wasn't to her. *It wasn't to her.*

'Oh, Neal, please take me back. *Please!*' she pleaded.

'That's not what you said to Stuart, I bet.' Neal's grin had a hard slant to it. He took the nose of the plane up with relentless satisfaction and told her, 'Sit tight, kitten, we've a long ride ahead of us.'

Because there was nothing she could do Laraine pointedly allowed the noise of the engine to separate her from the aggravating figure at the controls. At lunch time Neal informed her, 'There's a flask and sandwiches in a bag on the seat behind.'

She seethed afresh at this new realisation that he had known when he left the house that he was going to abduct her in the plane.

It was necessary to rise to reach over to the back seat. She had long since flicked out of the restricting seat belt. The flight had been smooth, but when she was turning back with the bag in her hand the floor tilted slightly and she was flung against Neal.

She clambered to an upright postion, steeling herself against the painfully sweet feel of his nearness and glowered, 'You did that on purpose, and if you say Scout's honour"——!'

He met her gaze his own lazily amused one, showing no trace of apology.

They flew over scenery that drew Laraine's eye despite her annoyance. A line of islands stretched away to the north-west. Many were visible peaks of mountains rising for thousands of feet from the ocean floor, others just hummocks in a few feet of water. But it was the Banks from which these hummocks rose, vast plateaus of sand, thousands of square miles in extent, which made a fascinating tapestry of sun-shot golds and clearwater silvers under the intense blue of the sky. The circular, cavernous depths of blue holes were clearly visible in stretches of sea, making Stuart an almost tangible presence in the tiny cabin of the aircraft.

Laraine had become so interested in the view she hadn't noticed that they were beginning to lose height. But when Neal banked and took them down to where a group of white-sanded cays lay like a string of pearls on fluorescent green silk she tensed anew in her seat.

As they descended the beaches of the island they were making for showed themselves to be completely deserted. There were snug anchorages, but no boats! Piles of conch shells on the sand, but no fishermen. There were supposed to be scattered native settlements this way, she was sure, but from what she could see from palm treetop heights, coconuts in profusion speeding by the plane's undercarriage the place looked alarmingly devoid of life.

They came down on an open stretch of ground which Neal at the controls of his Cherokee aircraft took to like a second home, and which told Laraine with sickening clarity that he had been here before. Stepping out, one's nose was assailed by the fresh, biting scent of open seas, and closer at hand the earthy warmth of tropical vegetation and island fertility.

Laraine had toyed with the idea of staying put inside the plane, but the threatening glint in Neal's eyes as he reached to give her a hand had put paid to that.

He led the way across the clearing and Laraine had no option but to follow, for the eerie loneliness of the place set her nerves twanging and Neal was, after all, a comfort in that sense. Adele would have suffered no such misgivings, of course. Neal would have transported her in his arms to the snug place he was leading the way to now, and it was this thought that kept Laraine tremulously a good half-dozen paces behind the menacing width of those broad shoulders.

Neal looked back and said, 'As you can see, there's no danger of us starving here. The trees in these parts will supply us with papayas, tamarinds, oranges, sapodillas, bananas, plantains, mangoes, sugar apples, sea-grapes, genips, avocado pears—oh, and then there's fish. . . .' he went through every last item with a kind of cheerful re-assurance that put Laraine's teeth on edge. The idea of starving was not what worried her.

'You forgot to mention the coconuts,' she said sweetly in a spirited attempt to deflate some of his ego. But her words bounced off his inflexible hide and he merely bowed to her observation.

They were following a path through the trees that ran parallel with a gleaming white beach, glimpses of which could be spied through the boles of the palms. But it was what lay up ahead that made Laraine's heart thump quite noticeably against her ribs.

Coming into view now was a grass hut wearing a deserted air as though a long since gone Robinson Crusoe had once resided there. It was set in a little clearing of beaten earth and backed on to tumbling escarpments grown over with flaming red jungle flowers and leafy vines. The thatched roof was fringed in true paradise island style, and Laraine wondered with a stab of envy and misery how long it had taken Neal to put it together for his stay here with Adele.

The door was hinged with reed fibres and leaning open at an angle it showed a crude, sparsely furnished interior which evoked a sense of comfort and rough charm, something Laraine could not deny, though she would dearly have loved to see it as a hovel.

Neal had stopped to kick the refuse of rotting fruit away from the beaten earth surrounded, so she felt safe in taking a peep into the interior. But she wished she hadn't. There were things here that made her feel even more desolate inside—masculine oddments that she knew had some connection with Neal; a rug-covered couch, its mattress filled with sea-scented moss, no doubt, a solid reed-lathed table and coconut shell utensils arranged on palm-leaved shelf space.

'Very cosy!' Laraine hadn't meant the exclamation to escape from her lips, nor for it to sound so bitterly disparaging, but it had, and it was only just in time that she saw Neal making for the hut and was able to duck outside and put on a look of absorbed fascination at the overhead greenery.

'I'm glad you like it,' Neal said companionably.' We might be stuck here a while. I'm not sure I've got enough gas in the tank to get the Cherokee out of here.'

While he put the bags he had brought with him on the table and generally made himself at home inside the hut Laraine stood rooted, her face paling to the colour of the sand that twinkled through the trees. 'You can't be serious!' she croaked. 'You must have known how much fuel it would take to get us back to Nassau?'

'We'll see,' he shrugged contentedly. 'The Cherokee can be fitted with sea-skis so we can always take off over the waves, and if she comes down we'll just float around for a day or two until someone spots us.'

Laraine didn't know how much of his manner was meant to be teasing and how much was in deadly earnest, but she decided it would be wiser to make light of the matter. After all, there was something undeniably exciting about the idea of being stranded anywhere with Neal. If only—*if only* the circumstances were different!

She watched a column of ants making for a fallen cluster of mastic berries. When she turned Neal was emerging from the hut, a metal stick-like object in his hand. 'Well, time to be thinking about supper,' he said cheerfully. He had discarded his clothes and came padding by her in athletic-looking swim-shorts. 'Too bad you didn't have time to throw a few things in a case,' he lamented smilingly, 'but you had your chance and you muffed it. We could have kidded ourselves we were two castaways stuck with each other's company—but hardly complaining,' he tacked on with a lazy glint in his green eyes. 'As it is, you've only got the fancy clothes you're wearing, and if you get those wet. . . .'

Laraine forced her gaze into resting curiously on the crude weapon in his hand. Accommodatingly he explained, 'It's a spear-gun. A bit old-fashioned, I'll admit—the gun stock uses rubber bands to propel the spear—but we should manage to get something tasty for our first meal by starlight.'

He strolled off through the palms, and, left with the silence of the clearing made ominous by nearby scufflings in the trees, Laraine turned and hurried after him.

The beauty of the beach and its surroundings caught at her heart in a way that made her long for the days when she had been on a friendly footing with Neal. To be here alone with him and to be wrapped around with the old familiar warmth of his companionship was something she would have done anything to bring about. But they might have been on different planets now as she sat stiffly drawing patterns with her toes in the sand and he splashed and turned, making the most of the sun-gilded water before he dived to go fishing.

Without appearing to Laraine watched him cavorting

with annoying carefree abandon. Droplets of water showered like diamonds from his glistening copper physique. Framed against an endless expanse of ocean and cloud-flecked sky, he was a rugged islander in every sense of the word.

Dejectedly she found herself wondering if Adele had sat like this watching Neal perform. It was crazy, she knew, but she almost fancied she could smell her sister-in-law's expensive French perfume wafting on the breeze.

Colourful birds came to hop tamely on the sand. Against the westering sun the coconut palms were outlined in fiery gold. Laraine was likening it to another beach where a little dog usually trotted at their heels. Oh, it would all have been so perfect, but now it never could be. The ghost of Adele had seen to that. And there was Stephanie too.

Laraine had never been able to erase from her mind the memory of those tempestuous moments in Neal's arms that afternoon in his garden, but a bleak look towards the water told her that she had been wrong; that it had been foolish to let herself believe that she would accept Neal's nearness on any terms. She knew now that when you loved a man you would never be content with just the shell of him.

CHAPTER ELEVEN

Dusk was darkening the sky to a royal blue glow when Neal returned from his fishing expedition with a waving thing on the end of his spear. 'Spiny lobster makes good eating.' He tossed it at her feet with a businesslike grin. 'I've done the hunting, now you're in charge of the pot.'

She struggled to get to her feet as he moved off and asked, 'Wh-where are you going?'

'To take a stroll.'

'What, *now*!' Her eyes fastened on the shadows that were heralding the night.

'Relax, there's nothing to be scared of,' he said offhandedly. 'You're not likely to stumble across any wild animals, if that's what's worrying you. There's none, as far as I know, in these parts.'

'As far as you know?' Before she could think of any excuse to detain him he had propped his fishing tackle against the base of a palm where he could easily recover it and disappeared through the trees.

Laraine scrabbled to find her shoes, but it was useless, she knew, to think of catching up to him. And wandering alone through a darkening forest was not her idea of discovering the island's charm. She flopped down again on the sand, her chin in her hand in wordless exasperation.

The foam-filled breakers fell with increasing monotony over the dusk-shrouded beach. A star here and there flickered to gain attention in the tropical expanse of sky. All manner of sounds began to make themselves heard at her back among the tangle of trees; snufflings and twitters and ominous cracking of dry twigs.

The skin started to crawl at the nape of her neck. No matter what Neal had said, there was something back there—something on four legs, she was ready to swear! And here she was on the open beach, a sitting duck for anything that cared to come out and investigate her.

All of a sudden the hut seemed an inviting place. At least she would have four walls and a door to hint to the sniffing night marauders that she didn't care for their company. Shakily she put on her shoes and stumbled, panicking at every sound, along the path through the trees. The grass hut was but a blur in the clearing, but she homed in on it like a distraught pigeon seeking sanctuary from some hidden foe.

The door was alarmingly fragile and ineffective. She managed to wedge it shut at last, but a puff of breeze would have dislodged it, and it was possible to see and be seen through the frayed and uneven reed thonging that held it together.

How long had Neal been gone? Half an hour? An hour? He must have had time to explore the whole island by now. Sitting stiffly on the couch, Laraine altered her position several times, and once the silvery bauble of a rising moon winked at her through the chinks of the door.

She wanted to tell it to go away; that it was on the wrong set. This was no paradise island scene; not for her. This was a torment of being condemned to stay where Neal had made love to Adele.

But she couldn't shut out the view, though it would have meant merely shifting her position. Through the bright glisten of damp in her eyes she kept her gaze on the door, knowing that, as the moon continued to smile at her from its place through the trees, nothing could have been more heart-swellingly romantic.

A scuffle outside brought her mind back to more practical things. Practical in the sense that her nerves soared, triggering off a scream in her throat, and she was off the couch and pressing herself against the far wall of the hut in an attempt to put as much space as possible between herself and the disturbance. Whatever was out there was showing a blatant disregard for her safety precautions! She could hear the clunk-clunk of something against the hut, and not one but a series of movements in the surrounding bushes! *Oh, Neal, please come back!*

The crackling of a distant footstep alerted her anew. She hadn't expected to have her prayers answered so soon, and she peeped out sceptically, half expecting to come face to face with some yellow-eyed creature of the forest. But oh, joy! Oh, bliss! It *was* Neal, and in her relief she fell against the door. Almost losing her balance as it flimsily gave way prompted her to greet him accusingly, 'You had a nerve, going off and leaving me like that! I've been surrounded by all kinds of horrible roving night life!'

'Oh?' Neal's mouth quirked. 'Like wild cats and things?'

'How do I know?' she shrugged irritably, resisting an urge to run into his arms.

Instead she watched him advance, a tiny pulse hammering in her temple. Bare to the waist, he had on a pair of old cotton twill trousers acquired from heaven knew where. In the pale light of the clearing he really did look like some husky castaway come home after foraging.

'Where's supper?' he asked. 'That spiny lobster should be cooked to a turn by now.'

'Of course I haven't done anything,' she scoffed impatiently, thinking of the unfortunate crustacean still lying on the beach. The whole trip had never been a game to her, and knowing suddenly that it was not that any more to Neal she backed into the hut and said swallowingly, 'I don't know how far you intend to take this thing. . . .'

'To the bitter end,' he replied glintingly, following her inside. As she faced him uncertainly he added with a bent smile,' With your new-found sophistication you should easily be able to cope with a situation like this.'

Wishing this were so but clinging to the part anyway, she was fired to reply, 'Are we all grown up, then? Personally I prefer my men a little bit more removed from the boyish prank stage.'

He didn't lose his smile, but it hardened somewhat, and only an arm's length away he asked, 'Is that why you're infatuated with Stuart?'

For a moment his remark floored her, then her exasperation returned and she said with a disbelieving laugh, 'Why is everybody so convinced that Stuart is a villain?'

'You didn't know him in his younger days,' said Neal, 'when he lived at a pace that left most of the other hell-raisers standing.'

'Well, I know him now, and what I know I like,' Laraine retorted.

'And that of course explains why you didn't care for the idea of him going away with Adele'

Laraine had only been stating an honest fact in her last

remark, but now she saw where it was leading her. However, she was borne along by this familiar feeling of power she had discovered when withholding certain information—so she countered sweetly, 'Who told you that?'

'It was more than obvious last night at the party.' Neal moved in an inch. 'The way you dolled yourself up for Stuart's benefit stood out a mile.'

Resentment suddenly burgeoned in Laraine, laying low every other emotion. To think that he thought . . . !

'Oh, you're so sure you know it all, aren't you?' she was stung to reply. 'Well, it may interest you to learn that Adele lent me that dress. She insisted that I wear it for the dinner party at Medway.'

'You're not afraid of Adele.' Neal was sceptical. 'You didn't have to conform to her demands.'

True, Laraine was bound to admit. Why had she done it, then? Giving it some thought, she supposed it was with the sneaking hope that Neal would find her attractive in the dress.

This wistful lapse spent mooning over last night put her off her guard and before she knew where she was Neal had taken her in his arms. 'We're wasting time with preliminaries,' he said with a wolfish smile. 'You may not be agreeable to the pact, but you're part of it, and we're committed to follow this through.'

'Neal, I've just had a thought!' she mentioned brightly. 'I *could* cook the lobster. I don't know about seasoning, but I'm sure it would turn out delicious if——'

'Your response as a matey castaway is disappointing,' he said laconically, not easing the tightness of his arms around her in any way.

The wistfulness was like a tear in her throat, but she managed to retort,' Well, I'm sorry if I don't have Adele's kind of welcoming approach.'

'Ah, Adele!' he said absently chasing Laraine's lips with his own and suffocating her with his wildly exciting nearness.

Avoiding his mouth while watching it hypnotically, she grasped at an old strength and said with a hysterical laugh, 'And I was thinking of Stuart! This is a mad set-up. It ought to be the other way round.'

She thought her spine would snap then in the intensity of his embrace. There were quizzical sparks of fire in his green eyes as he murmured, 'But we agreed to do a swop, three against one, so I'm afraid you'll have to put up with me, my sweet.' He made the term of endearment sound like a caress, mimicking Stuart's style of delivery, in a way that made Laraine fume. With a sinking feeling that she was not going to be able to break free from his hold or leave the hut tonight, she closed her eyes for a moment to cope with the waft of sweet pain at his nearness. Then, opening them, she blazed, while renewing her struggles, 'I used to think you were a man worth knowing, Neal Hansen, but now. . . .'

He fixed her with a look of twinkling irony. 'I might still be if you'd give this castaway idea a chance.'

'I've no intention of falling in with the bored schemes of the rich!' She sidetracked his descending lips with a jerk of her head.

'But you didn't mind indulging Stuart's whims and slipping off on a trip away from Nassau?'

'Why shouldn't I? You were busy doing the same with the fourth member of the quartet.' Her flash of defiance was shortlived, for his lips were dangerously near the warm hollow of her throat. 'Neal,' meeting his gaze, she pleaded, 'please let me go.'

'Afraid, little one?' His tones were unexpectedly gentle, the light in his eyes almost teasing in a granite kind of way as he tacked on,' We're a long way from the schoolroom now.'

Laraine felt she would hit him if he didn't stop tormenting her with this worn-out theme. Given the chance, that was, for her arms were pinioned against her, Neal's being the most powerful by far. But she still had some breath and she used it scathingly with, 'Everyone's always telling me how juvenile I am, but for childish practice I reckon this latest fiasco of swopping partners is——'

'Now it's no use cribbing just because you were outvoted.'

This time Laraine couldn't, or wouldn't, avoid his lips, but just before their fusing with hers she came to enough to snap angrily, the tears in her eyes due mainly to her own weakness, 'Pact or no pact, I never thought you'd have the gall to bring me to the same little love-nest you shared with Adele!'

Neal's dark head, which had been lowering intently, suddenly stopped and lifted. 'Adele?' He voiced the name as though he was taking note of it for the first time. Then with an oblique grin he said, 'Adele's never been here.'

Of course Laraine didn't believe this. Hadn't she detected whiffs of Adele's perfume on the island? Or had that been imagination? She stared somewhat and accused, 'But you went away with her. You flew out of Nassau with her, I know you did,'—she had sniffed Adele's perfume in the plane, that *definitely* hadn't been imagination—'to some desert island where you were going to go native for a while, wasn't that how she put it?'

'Oh, that!' Neal looked vague. 'Yes, I remember. But we only got as far as Cat Island. Adele had some friends at the Cutlass Bay Hotel whom she wanted to see again. I dropped her off there and took the Cherokee for a check-up to a servicing hangar north of the island. I didn't get to pick Adele up until the following afternoon.'

Laraine had gone quite limp in his arms. Her mind was trying to grasp at this shining piece of news which she didn't dare to believe that she had heard correctly. 'You mean . . . there was no hideaway love-nest, no native paradise?'

'Not unless the pool of the Cutlass Hotel fits that category,' Neal grinned. 'I had a dip there with some of Adele's friends before we left for Nassau.'

He had been viewing the change in her with a curious look in his eyes. Close enough at the moment to read her soul, it seemed, he was aware of the smoothing out of something in her lavender blue gaze; of a veiled radiance which was in danger of lighting up her young features. And he watched all this with something like bemusement in his own expression.

But after the first flush of riotous happiness Laraine was once again seized with annoyance. The fact that he had tortured her and tormented her all this time, leading her to believe, unwittingly or not, that he had slipped away to some isolated haven with Adele, was to her mind unforgivable. Those long days and nights of pure misery were with her as she said with brassy humour, 'No wonder the two of you were so put out because Stuart and I really did go to a magical isle!'

Neal's gaze was twin spots of green flame in the darkness. His arms became steel bands as he told her, 'But it's not you and Stuart now. It's you and me, and for tucked-away privacy this beats the shoreside digs on Cat Cay, I bet.'

Laraine was enjoying easing her annoyance. The feeling outweighed any misgivings she might have concerning the menacing light in his eyes, and airily she dreamed aloud, 'It was a night I'll never forget. Stuart turned out to be the perfect beach cottage companion——'

'Well, let's see if we can follow his example——' Neal had swung her up into his arms and the covered couch was ominously near. As she bounced on the mattress and his rugged form came looming in she panicked sufficiently to blurt, 'I was going to say——'

'You were going to say——?' Neal's mouth came down hard on hers. She fought for breath. 'I was going to say,' she gasped, 'that he—simply talked and talked—about his love life with June Shor—and like a good friend let me have the bedroom, while he doffed down on the beach——' She couldn't get the words out quick enough.

'So now we have it!' Neal's eyes glinted in the shadows. There was a curious smile on his lips as though he too had known a certain amount of torment.

Both of them were breathing fast, but gazing up at him Laraine was suddenly conscious of a suspended moment between them; one that seemed to stretch away into eternity, so infinite in depth was its unspoken message.

Laraine wanted this powerfully sweet sensation to go on for ever. It was Neal who broke the spell. 'I thought I'd wring the truth out of you one way or another,' he said, jerking her to a sitting position. 'You've been just a bit too cock-a-hoop for my liking these past few days.'

Laraine didn't believe she had been any such thing. And really it was her turn now to be bemused. Had it meant so much to Neal, the discovery that she and Stuart were just friends?

She moved to lean her back against the wall of the hut and drawing up her knees under her chin she said impishly, 'Just put it down to my impatience to appear worldly-wise.'

It was funny. They had wrestled at kissing distance, each believing the worst about the other, but now that it had turned out to be all so much hot air, there was a curious distance between them. But not an unpleasant one.

Neal said, eyeing her with a grin, 'You know, I think we will have that lobster stew. There's some herbs and peppers we could use and with the fruit growing around here I reckon we could produce quite a banquet.'

'Mmmm!' Laraine realised she was famished and leapt from the couch, eager to start.

Her arms were loaded with food bowls and eating utensils from the shelves. 'We'll go to the beach,' said Neal, sorting out a makeshift stewpan to add to his own pile and other items that would prove useful. 'It will make a more spacious living room, and we'll plug into the moon for light for the table.'

Laraine laughed, her chin balancing her oddments. As their glances met she supposed he was thinking she was too cock-a-hoop again. Well, could she help it if her eyes were shining?

The moon really did look like a friendly lantern suspended above a throne of silver cloud as they spread their things on the sand. Neal went to gather wood and made a fire from matches produced out of a waterproof tin. The little grass hut seemed remarkably well equipped, Laraine thought in passing. She had a bad moment when she realised they had no fresh water for cooking, but Neal, returning along the path, produced this too, which convinced her that their little paradise was just about perfect. She would call it Dream Island, she decided, viewing the sentinel palms frosted with moonlight and the pewter waves falling on the beach, because all at once it was a dreamy place to be.

When the dining area was set and a bowl of limes and sea-grapes and mangoes added the finishing touch Neal said, giving the contents of the can over the fire a stir with chef-like satisfaction, 'There's nothing to do now but wait. You can't rush good cooking.'

Laraine looked around her, stretched in the clothes she had worn since early that morning, and spoke recklessly. 'I want to swim. It's all right for you, you've managed to wash away the dust of travel.'

'Don't blame me because you didn't bring a swimsuit,' he gleamed at her.

'No, I didn't, but I don't intend to let that stop me,' she said over her shoulder, making for the shadows of the palms. What she was wearing under her blouse and slacks was a lot more than some of the brief bikinis one saw on the beaches these days, and like a silvery sprite in the moon's radiance she raced to meet the waves.

In the warm night air the seas was like anointing oil on her skin. She submerged slowly, laughing at the cool, creeping delight which stole up her body, then struck out with strong strokes over the mirror-like surface. She felt exalted enough to take on the world, and as she floated on her back, gazing up at the star-studded heavens, it did seem as though she held it in the palm of her hand.

Deep laughter mingled with hers as Neal stripped down

to swimming trunks and came to join her. They swam like a pair of dolphins with the crescent of ivory beach and dark fringe of overhanging palms as their audience. And later, floating in their little lagoon, they could see the homely red glow of the fire on the beach and the vapour of cooking like white mist in the moonlight.

'Supper should be about ready,' said Neal. 'We ought to be getting back.'

'You go,' Laraine laughed. 'I'm going to swim alongside the beach for a while and then run back. I've got to get my clothes dry somehow.'

'Nothing doing.' Neal shoved his hair out of his eyes and turned with her. 'I'm not leaving you in the water on your own. Come on! By the time we've done this stint we should really be as hungry as a couple of castaways.'

With a whoop he led the way and, choking with the giggles, because it wasn't easy to swim when pure unadulterated happiness hampered her breathing, she splashed alongside. On the beach Neal also had the advantage over her and, sprinting, he had reached the fire before she was halfway along the coral strand. Coming up breathlessly behind, she was satisfied to notice that her panties and bra were drying fast. He tossed her a towel as she reached the palm shadows and draping it like a sarong around her body she felt exhilarated, refreshed and hungry.

The thing that had look so dull and uninteresting lying on the sand earlier turned out to be the most delicious spiny lobster that Laraine had so far tasted. She wanted to know the secret of Neal's culinary magic, but tantalisingly he told her as they ate, 'It's a little thing I learned as a boy when we were out with the sloops. Diving for sponges was fun and when we wanted to eat we'd just beach the boats wherever it happened to be handy. Some of the old-timers knew tricks about cooking seafood that had been handed down to them from the days of the first seafarers in the Bahamas. It's all to do with the clever use of herbs, you see. I and my pals soon got pretty nifty with a stewpot ourselves, but there's a rule among the old-timers in the fishing fraternity, and outside of it we're committed not to divulge what we know.'

'Cheek!' grinned Laraine, scooping up a tasty morsel. 'How can they expect their womenfolk to be good cooks if they withhold all the answers?'

'We've got to reserve some small independence, otherwise our women would get too stroppy for their own good.' Neal's smile was a merry one.

There were biscuits left over from lunch on the plane and the fruit proved to be an abundant filler. When they were rounding off the meal with cool coconut milk drunk from shells sliced deftly in half by a handy tool from Neal's grass hut store, Laraine asked dreamily, 'And the boys who went diving for sponges with you. Where are they now?'

Neal shrugged. 'Grown up and married, most of them, with families of their own. One or two of them got jobs in the States and some have built homes on neighbouring islands. Tom Laxalt, a special pal of mine, runs a beach café with his wife over at Coral Harbour on New Providence. Their three youngsters help out at the tables. And Chick Wasey, my team mate at college, runs a coconut estate with his family on Eleuthera. We run into one another occasionally.'

'Don't you feel you're missing something when you see them—settled down, I mean?' Laraine toyed with the milky flesh of her coconut.

'I haven't done up to now,' came the reply.

She looked across at him, and the stars lit the mischief in her eyes as she asked, 'Up to now? You mean . . . right this minute?'

'That sounds like an angling kind of question to me.' His own eyes in the silvery light were pinpoints of humour.

'But you haven't answered it,' she persisted impishly. Broad of shoulder in his castaway trousers, Neal eyed her where she sat in her towelled sarong. After a long moment he drawled, 'And you needn't think because you're sitting there as demure as an island flower that I'm going to. Go and get dressed.'

'Yes, Neal.' She rose meekly, but shining-eyed, and padded away to the trees.

The only thing that was damp about her now was her hair, and running her fingers through it when she had donned slacks and blouse was enough, she guessed, to set it to rights. When she returned to the fire Neal was lounging with his back propped against the plane bags and the pile of oddments from the grass hut. He beckoned her lazily to join him and, chic now, she considered, in her tailored blue slacks and cap-sleeved white blouse, she nestled down beside him.

They were facing the sea and everything was curiously still. Only the moon climbed his starry highway, his cloak of silver trailing over the whispering waves. Contentedly Laraine said, 'Our very own paradise island! It truly is, isn't it, Neal?'

He didn't answer immediately, and when he did it was not quite in reply to her question. 'You don't look exactly like a left-over from a shipwreck at the moment,' he said drily, 'you're too out of character in your smart get-up.'

'I had to do something to shake off the little girl image you've been labelling me with.' She raised her chin at him. Then wriggling her bare feet next to his in the sand and recalling the somewhat tempestuous tussle in the grass hut, she dared to tease, 'Wasn't it you who said we're a long way from the schoolroom now?'

'Guilty,' he grinned. He was very close to her and looking deep into her eyes he became suddenly serious. His lips came down on hers, gently, tenderly, lovingly almost, but in a way that left her vaguely unsatisfied, and though her heart was pounding with the joy of his nearness, she found herself asking wonderingly when he finally drew away, 'What was that for?'

'You didn't deserve the manhandling I gave you in the garden at my place that day,' he said in deep tones. 'You're a sweet kid—ah, sorry!—a sweet young lady—and I've been meaning to apologise for some time.'

'I'm sorry you've waited so long,' Laraine said huskily.

Whether by accident or design he was still very close to her. From somewhere in the region of her bare throat she snatched at his lips with her own and all about made sweet contact. Neal didn't hurry from where their mouths flirted, the brush of a kiss away, but after a long lingering moment he said gruffly, 'Apologies over,' and straightening added obscurely, 'I don't care what the law says, you're still a minor to me—understand?'

'Yes, Neal,' Laraine replied obediently, but wildly happy. His next words, however, plunged her into a maelstrom of puzzlement and uncertainty that was like a dash of cold water after the near realisation of her dreams.

'Besides,' Neal was saying, jabbing at the dying embers of the fire with energy, 'I don't want to be accused of encroaching on young McKelway's property.'

'Conrad?' Laraine looked blank. 'How did he get into this thing?' She hadn't given the young Naval officer a thought for some days, though vaguely at the back of her mind she knew that he was due in Nassau for a stretch of leave any time now.

'Don't ask me why,' Neal's mouth was wry, 'but I appear to have got stuck with the role of guardian where you're concerned.'

'Well?' She waited.

'You've seen quite a lot of young Conrad in the past, haven't you?' said Neal.

'I suppose I have,' she paused to think. 'We often met at the Reef Club when Adele wanted to spend the afternoon there, and he's always dropping in at Medway when he's free, but——'

'So you must have got to know each other pretty well?'

'You could say that . . .' Laraine was remembering the long summer afternoons she had spent with Conrad on the beach and in the grounds of Medway. They had had fun together, mainly because she had worked hard at trying to forget about Neal and Adele left to themselves on the veranda. In a detached sort of way she had grown fond of Conrad, but she didn't see why she should be reminded of that now.

Not so much out of curiosity as to even up her shaky heartbeats she asked, 'Why are we discussing Conrad?'

'Don't you know?' Neal's eyes held a subtle gleam.

'Should I?' A silly little pulse bothered her in her throat.

Neal stretched his legs. 'Young Mister McKelway comes from good Naval stock, as you probably know.' Laraine did, though she had only listened with half an ear to Conrad's eager chat concerning his background. 'He belongs to a family who still retain certain old-world courtesies, and with the respect which is an admirable side to his make-up he came over and asked me, before he left on this latest sea job, if it would be all right if you and he became engaged when he returns to Nassau on leave.'

'Engaged?' Laraine blinked. She recalled now how Conrad, during his most recent visits to Medway, before he had gone off on this latest charting exercise, had talked to her with a tender look in his eyes. But she had been a little distracted by thoughts of Neal and Stuart, who had not been on speaking terms at the time.

'I think that's the idea.' Neal sloped a smile.

'But I don't love Conrad.' She looked at him pointedly. She might have made some passing remark about the weather.

'He's the right man for you.' Neal poked at the fire. 'He's got a good solid position, and an expensive background. You won't want for anything, I'm sure of that, and as husbands go he'll be pretty devoted.'

Belligerent, hurt and muddled and with a dawning realisation, she jerked upright to confront him. 'Oh? And you think that's basis enough for a happy marriage?' She spoke to his granite profile. 'Just because you've been let down by a woman you think there's no such thing as true love—well, I know there is.'

He turned his head and challenged with a hollow laugh, 'Oh? And how do you know that?'

Drowning in his gaze, she wanted to remind him of a certain look they had shared in the confines of the grass hut, but up against a kind of relentless humour in him she could only reply stubbornly, 'I just do, that's all.'

'Well, we'll see,' Neal said with finality. 'McKelway will be back in Nassau in a few days and I'll be around to give him my reply. In the meantime we'd better see about bedding down for the night.' He rose. 'We'll get this gear back to the hut and I'll rig up some kind of sleeping accommodation in the clearing. You can have the couch in the hut.'

Laraine carried an armful of clutter back through the trees dutifully, and not unhappily. The heady wonder of all that had transpired during the evening between her and Neal was still a warm glow in her mind. And she would go on calling it her dream island. She would!

CHAPTER TWELVE

WHEN they were settled for the night she said worriedly, poking her head out of the hut doorway for the last time, 'Are you sure you're going to be all right just lying there? There's all kinds of prowling beasts in the forest, you know. I've heard them.'

'Yeah, you told me,' said Neal, gazing at the stars. Laraine couldn't swear to it, but she thought she detected amusement in his tones. So he thought she was imagining things, did he?! Well, he would soon see. She closed the flimsy door on herself with trepidation and groped for the couch. It had been an eventful day and even the idea of four-legged marauders paying her a call could not keep her from drifting off into blissful sleep.

But perhaps she had had them on her mind even in oblivion, for the first sound she heard when she awoke to find the early morning sunshine slanting through the gaps in the hut was the familiar thump-thump and rustle-rustle of something outside. She didn't wait to find out if it was part of her dreams, she was sure it wasn't anyway, and scrambling off the couch she ran screaming out of the hut, 'Neal!'

He was giving himself a leisurely shave beside a mirror he had propped in the fork of a tree, and as he caught her close in his arms some of the frothy soap from his chin somehow got transferred to cheeks. 'I told you!—didn't I *tell* you!' She pointed with a shaky finger which soon began to lower limply as she looked across the clearing, eventually taking the whole length of her accusing arm with it.

'I forgot to mention,' Neal said with a grin,' we're only a short way from a native settlement here.'

'Goats!' Laraine exclaimed in disgust. 'And chickens!' She watched the strutting, feathered fowls, feeling slightly ridiculous. 'Do you mean to say . . . ?'

There was no need to go on. Neal's face was a study in suppressed laughter, and it wasn't long before she was infected by the hilarity of it all. Wild cats indeed! But then her lavender blue eyes became big and serious and she murmured, 'So it's not a paradise island?'

'It is in a way,' Neal reassured her. 'This cay is one of the Exhumas which extend for something like a hundred miles. The chain is uninhabited except for widely scattered native settlements where life remains simple, almost unchanged from Colonial days.' He cleaned his chin and pointed through the trees. 'A short way over the ridge are some of the houses of the community of this island, which is known as Little Farmers' Cay.'

Laraine watched the goats scrounging for succulent scraps of vegetation and realised that their blunderings against the grass hut had been the cause of all those strange sounds she had heard last night. She cast a glance around, recalling all the home comforts that had been miraculously on hand for their desert island stay. Of course, she should have known that all these fruit trees and the beachside cultivation had not happened by accident. And then there was the grass hut, stocked with handy tools and useful equipment.

As though he read her mind Neal said with a wicked expression, 'I've been coming here since I was a boy. It's a handy spot for fishing and being with one's own thoughts for a while. In the past, when I've been able to take a break from things, I've lived here for five or six weeks at a stretch.' With the towel he was holding he brushed the soapy foam from Laraine's face and explained, 'Remember that first day when we were chasing Woodes in the back meadow? Well, Abraham—he was the one with the rake—lives on Little Farmers' Cay. He was visiting relatives at the time at my place. Jordan, Jemima and the rest, they're all family with roots in Little Farmers'. Anyway, Abe looks after the hut here for me and cleans it out every once in a while. I like to keep things as simple as possible and Abe understands and doesn't try to fancy things up. He and his family leave me to it when I'm here and that's the way I like it; although they're great ones for hospitality when they get the chance. Which reminds me,' Neal tidied a stray lock away from her temple and tweaked up the collar of her blouse, 'better find those shoes of yours. They're expecting us for breakfast.'

'Expecting us?' Laraine blinked.

'I took a walk over there last night while you were coping with the local jungle beasts,' Neal quipped. 'I told them about you—that I had a guest.' He tucked his shirt down his linen beach slacks. 'You don't mind, do you?'

Mind! At the moment Laraine's face was reminiscent of the radiant look she had worn last night. Neal had brought her here to his sacred domain. She was the only one he had allowed into this retreat of his away from the world. Was it surprising then that her heart was singing fit to burst?

She skipped to get her shoes, and brushing down her clothes, happily quite wrinkle-free despite the fact that she had slept as she was, she said gaily, 'What do you suppose they'll give us for breakfast? I'm starving!'

'The inevitable conch or crab chowder,' Neal joked, indicating the way. 'The folks here rely on the sea for everything. And, of course, oranges, papayas, bananas, sapodillas. . . .'

'Don't start that again!' she giggled, watching her footing in her unsuitable shoes. His own amusement showing, he took her hand and they set off through the trees.

The houses of Little Farmers' Cay were clustered on a slope overlooking the vast Atlantic Ocean. Simple frame constructions, they were mostly painted white with gay red or dove-grey roofs, and fronted with wooden verandas which looked homely and inviting perched above the busy little harbour.

Laraine wondered why she hadn't seen all this activity when they had been coming in to land, but because of the great swathes of coconut palms and Neal's cleaver flying it had all been conveniently hidden from view.

She met Abraham again, a tall, well-built man who showed none of the aggressiveness he had displayed with the garden rake that day on Neal's property, Laraine thought, with silent laughter. Rather, his smile in his chocolate-coloured features was so wide one was reminded of the gleaming white boats floating hull-on in the harbour. He and his family couldn't do enough for her and Neal, and later they joined in the general trek to the beach where everybody was busy with some chore or another.

Laraine helped to weave palm-rib baskets which, weighted with a stone and dropped to the sea bottom, would serve as traps for groper and snapper. Neal, his trousers rolled up to the shins like hers, trimmed sponges along with the other men and sacked them ready for shipment. It was a sparkling day of laughter and mild confusion at the local dialect.

Laraine heard such expresssions as, 'Tie me loose, boss,' when someone wanted to cast off in a boat, and, 'She ain't fetched yet,' when another one hadn't arrived. The women, for all their merry way, were superstitious and would suddenly stop in the midst of chatter and say, 'Don't put mouth on it,' when they didn't want something to be mentioned for fear of bringing bad luck. And their idea of keeping quiet and staying out of trouble was described as 'shut mouth catch no fly.' But the expression that endeared the people of Little Farmers' Cay to Laraine most of all was one to do with their livelihood the sea. When a boat was sailing fast they said it was 'bruising God's waters.'

It was late afternoon when she and Neal finally returned to collect their things from the grass hut. Laraine had brought no luggage and Neal's consisted of no more than a couple of plane bags. The little palm-fringed hut was left to itself once again and they found the Cherokee waiting like a faithful friend in the clearing. Aware now that there was all the fuel one needed down at the fishing port, Laraine twinkled accusingly as Neal assisted her into the plane, 'You knew all along that there was no danger of us being stranded here.'

'None at all,' he winked. 'And I didn't mention either the Cherokee's two-way radio. We could have got in touch with someone in the area, a boat even. Stu and I often have a natter together when he's in the *Melanie* and I'm flying over the waves.'

His blithe way of informing her of this prompted her to comment with amused disgust, 'Putting the wind up me like that! I've a good mind not to talk to you on the journey back.' But she knew she would. To cut herself off from Neal, even jokingly, would be like shutting off the lifeblood to her heart.

Violet strands of night were garlanding Nassau harbour as they flew over on the way back to Medway. Neal landed on the strip beside his house and took Laraine back by road in his car. They found only Benjamin in the rambling old residence. Adele and Stuart hadn't returned.

Two days later Laraine found herself still the sole guest at Medway. But she was happy enough filling in the time until her sister-in-law's return. She had the freedom of the house and grounds and the beach was always a lovely place to wander. But best of all she could spend long sessions with Woodes. Neal worked on his land and sometimes he joined them for a picnic on the beach, or a stroll through the wooded sections of his estate. These occasions, of course, were the ones that made Laraine's heart swell with contentment.

Sometimes she spared an anxious thought for Adele, wondering if she was making more heartache for herself staying away with Stuart like this. But for the most part the sheer joy of being free to spend as much time as she liked out of doors and at Neal's place more than made up for the unease she felt at her sister-in-law's absence.

One afternoon Neal came in the back gate where she was teaching Woodes to sit until she called him; no easy feat, for, an excitable bundle, he leapt up and made to dash after her before she had taken half a step. 'I think we'll give work a miss for the rest of the day,' said Neal with humour at her hopeless task. And wiping his hands on the well rag, 'How would you like to come with me on a trip to town? I've got to order some cotton stock and fertilizer, and later we could see something of the Colonial charm of Nassau from a tourist buggy.'

'Oh, Neal, that would be lovely!' Laraine got to her feet, her eyes shining. 'When do I have to be ready?'

'I'll pick you up after lunch,' he grinned indulgently.

Laraine had never had time to explore Nassau—on her trips to town the long lists of requests that Adele gave her made such recreation impossible. But she was glad now that this had been the case, for what better person to see the sights with than Neal! And seated beside the man she loved how could it not prove to be a vivid experience?

In the back of their frosted-pink horse-drawn carriage with its frilled sun-roof they were transported at clip-clop pace by a native driver whose beaming lethargy was typical of the sun-soaked island. Laraine had put on her dress patterned with rosebuds, while Neal looked ruggedly attractive in a white town suit.

Along ancient streets lined with quaint whitewashed and latticed old homes and buildings, he told her a lot about history-rich Nassau, haunt of rum-soaked sailors and dashing pirates of the past. In contrast the straw markets were a delight in up-to-the-minute designs in hats, handbags and countless other accessories handmade by Bahamian craftsmen.

Neal made her laugh by trying on straw hats that changed his identity dramatically, from bank manager on holiday to beachcombing enthusiast. But Laraine was more fortunate in her choice. She tried on a hat which was the height of nonsense. Of close-fitting white straw with a narrow brim, its high crown was decorated with a pair of pink hands and gold bells. One of the hands was holding a wine glass close to the crown, which had the appearance of being half full of green liquid! Funnily enough the hat had a certain elegance. Neal liked her in it, and he bought it at once from the chuckling stallholder who had joined in the fun.

They went along the waterfront where sailboats were unloading fruit and vegetables from the out-islands, and vendors dozed under gay umbrellas in between sales of produce hauled for generations to market in this manner. Laraine was familiar with Bay Street, for with its international shops, Paris fashions, watches, crystal and china, this was where Adele was attracted to on their visits to Nassau.

Woodes Rogers Walk was what pleased Laraine more. Apart from it being named after the first Royal Governor of the Bahamas, *and* the namesake of their dog, hers and Neal's, she liked to think happily, it was one of the most colourful scenes in Nassau. A continuation of the waterfront where one could purchase fresh fish, fruit and vegetables, it was here where the Bahamian fishermen hauled in the day's catch while swopping fishing stories, and mended their nets on the crushed shell beach.

When they returned to the square with its statue of Queen Victoria and its impressive government offices, Laraine thought that was the end of the tour, but then Neal leaned forward and gave the driver an address. Later when they were ambling along a white road which climbed away into distant greenery, and where flaming bougainvillea and hibiscus tumbled over white wooden fences, Neal said lazily, 'I thought our present mode of transport would be a fitting way to call on old Adam while we're in town.'

Adam Webber! The tall military-looking man who had eyed Neal with such paternal affection that afternoon at the Coral Reef Country Club. Laraine sat up in her seat.

The old Colonel's house was just as Neal had described it to her. Tall with grey-tiled roof, its upstairs ironwork veranda painted green and white looked out on to the road, and the white-framed windows' green shutters made a pleasing contrast against strawberry pink walls.

Indoors it appeared that they were expected. In a room where heavy lace curtains shrouded the windows and china tea-set and tray rested on a lace-clothed round table, the atmosphere was one of Colonial elegance. The Colonel, resembling a Southerner of the United States with his tailored frock-coat and narrow trousers in pale fawn, greeted Laraine, his thin, cold hands gripping hers warmly. 'Now this is the young lady who sat as quiet as a mouse while everyone was yattering their heads off, that day at the Reef Club. I wondered when you were going to bring her along to see me, young feller.'

'I told you we'd get round to it,' Neal smiled idly.

'I've been biding my time,' old Adam winked. 'I saw the way your arrival on the scene that afternoon put roses into her cheeks.'

Laraine felt her face pinking over, but luckily the two men went on to talk about other matters, and later when it was left to her to pour the tea she was able to accomplish the feat with a steady hand and a happy smile playing around her lips.

Their host, with his clipped, military air and fierce white moustache, was such a colourful character Laraine was eager to hear something of his adventures in the field of war. Neal hinted as much, and when old Adam began to tell her of a time in the steaming jungles of Borneo she almost clapped her hand to her mouth in laughing surprise. Such was the Colonel's romantic appearance that Laraine had foolishly connected him with happenings during the Civil War in America. But though he was pretty ancient she realised now he would have to be a ghost to have taken part in such events, and this he certainly was not, as his exciting accounts of last stands against the Japanese proved.

As they had come to the house in one of the tourists' horse-drawn carriages, Neal was obliged to walk to town to pick up the car. He left Laraine in the Colonel's care, or it could have been the other way round, for as they walked out of doors to a table and chairs in the garden, he leaned on her young shoulder rather than use his stick over the uneven crazy paving.

She wouldn't have minded if Adam had wanted to continue with his sagas of modern warfare, although it was not nearly as exciting as delving into the rich, vibrant and sometimes violent past of Nassau with its blockade runners of the American Civil War, and the rum-runners of the

Prohibition era. However, the Colonel was a shrewd judge of audience and he proved that he was a listener too. As they sat viewing the flowery stretches and idly exchanging comments about the island he eyed Laraine rather keenly. Before she knew where she was she was talking about herself.

She told him about Richard, unemotionally now for she could talk about him in the detached way of someone long gone but lovingly remembered. And he listened intently, making no superfluous statements that would have brought tears to her eyes. She made little mention of Adele except as to her own connection with Richard's widow, for Adam obviously recalled with beetling brows Adele's gossiping behaviour that afternoon at the Reef Club and he was openly impatient on hearing her name.

Laraine couldn't ever remember talking to anyone with such depth about her life as she was doing now, and she felt an odd affinity for this erect old man who held Neal in such warm regard. He watched her not unkindly, but as though he would know the working of her mind.

When Neal returned she felt lighter of spirit and happier than she had ever been when Adam said, 'I suppose now you two young people are hankering to be off. Well, hear this, young feller—you bring Laraine to see me good and soon or I'll have your hide, understand?'

'We'll be along again some afternoon,' Neal said lazily. 'There's plenty of time, Adam.'

'For you, maybe, but there are things on this earth I've a mind to see settled before I go—and anyway,' the beetling brows came down over the prankish humour in his faded eyes, 'the girl's a flattering listener to the ramblings of an old fool like me.'

Laraine kissed him to show that she didn't think he was an old fool at all, and as he stood at the gate and watched them drive away there was a fierce brightness in his eyes.

Adele returned to Medway the following day. A new brilliance was in her eyes and she radiated a kind of breathless happiness which was destined to founder on the rocks of indifference. She said nothing of her days and nights away from New Providence.

Laraine was afraid that Adele's return would bring drastic changes to the pleasant rhythm of the two households, but for the moment anyway things stayed in a kind of limbo and she was able to come and go as she pleased. She loved her visits to Woodes and their hikes over the adjoining land, and she knew that Neal was working with a will in transforming his estate into cultivated stretches. Soon, she supposed, Stuart would want him again for the job of charting blue holes, but for the moment anyway there appeared to be no such intrusions in the blissful routine.

She didn't know then that looming on the horizon was a cataclysmic interruption, one that would put an abrupt end to all her wild imaginings where she and Neal were concerned.

The day started like any other, sunny and warm and full of promise. Ever after Laraine felt she would distrust any such sparkling morning because of what dark presentiments could lay hidden behind its glowing smile.

In the afternoon she made her customary trip over to see Woodes. Neal was supervising work on a strip on the south side bordering the beach. She knew that there was a chance that he would swim with her and Woodes if the work went well, and she was humming a tune under her breath as she fed the little dog scraps she had saved from her lunch.

The front of the house was miles away in her mind and she heard nothing of the arrival of the taxi or its departure. The only indication she had that there was someone in the house was when she heard a light step on the polished tiles. Absently she figured that it wouldn't be one of the servants, because the footsteps were crisply made on high heels, unless she was mistaken.

She didn't put herself out to go and see. It was not up to

her to make herself available to callers. But the lack of response to duties by native Bahamians in the heat of the afternoon was well known, and the next thing she knew the visitor had come right through to the outdoors and a laughing voice was asking, 'Is anybody at home?'

Laraine looked up to meet a pair of cinnamon-coloured eyes which in turn lowered over her in an offhand way, then she was being told, 'I'm Stephanie Keynes. Where's Neal?'

Stephanie! An ice-cold hand gripped Laraine's heart. The girl that Neal had never succeeded in putting out of his mind. She found her voice with difficulty and, aware of the rough simplicity of her beach attire against the tailored smartness of the visitor, she said, 'He's out working in the fields.'

'The fields?' the girl echoed with derogatory amusement which faded to impatience. 'Well, can't someone tell him I'm here?'

'I'll send one of the servants with a message,' Laraine said quickly, finding a lead for Woodes, who was bounding around the legs of the newcomer and making himself most unpopular. She put him in his kennel and went through the kitchen to the servants' quarters where Jemima despatched a fourteen-year-old nephew, fleet of foot, to inform the boss that he had a visitor.

There was nothing else for it then but to hang about uncomfortably. Stephanie Keynes, Laraine saw, was tallish, about Neal's height, with a neat figure and luxuriant hair the same colour as her eyes. She was attractive in a tawny kind of way, but there was something that Laraine couldn't take to in those eyes; a self-interested light, perhaps, a feeling that one could easily be deceived by the bland good nature that was displayed there.

She hadn't introduced herself, and to pass the time Stephanie asked without interest, 'Who are you?'

'Just a next-door neighbour,' Laraine shrugged. 'Neal looks after my dog for me. My sister-in-law won't have him in the house.'

'I don't blame her.' Stephanie spoke abstractedly, her mind obviously out there in the fields.

Much to Laraine's dejection Neal put in an appearance all too soon. 'Steve!' He came through the back gate with eyes only for her. 'When did you arrive in New Providence?'

'About an hour ago,' she laughed, embracing him. 'I took a taxi straight here. My bags are in the hall.'

He drew her arms down from around his neck and indicating the way said, 'Come on inside.'

Gulping, Laraine watched them go. Neal hadn't even noticed her. Feeling miserably superfluous about the place, she released Woodes, saw that he had fresh water for drinking, then closing the gate after her scuffed back to Medway.

She didn't say anything to Adele about their next-door visitor. Her sister-in-law was suspended in a dream world which had something to do with the introspective brilliance in her eyes. But she came to sufficiently, mainly because of an avid feminine interest, when Neal's guest arrived on the doorstep at Medway that same evening.

It was not late, but Adele had changed into one of her expensive negligés and was toying with the pages of a glossy magazine, attracted by the new range of perfumes which, if she decided to buy them would set her back a small fortune. Laraine, wearing a much-laundered dressing gown in forget-me-not blue, was curled up in an armchair trying to read a book. This fashion of spending the evening stemmed from the times when she would sit with pencil and notebook waiting for orders for the following day and to take down the numerous requests which Adele would invariably have in mind. But at the moment her sister-in-law was showing no drive for matters concerning the household or anything else, and so Laraine was sitting with her eyes on the print of her book while suffering torturing thoughts of Neal and Stephanie together in the house next door.

When the car stopped outside Benjamin was on hand to open the front door. Familiar with the routine of the house, Neal drifted straight through to the room with the picture window, Stephanie at his side. 'Sorry to barge in on you like this,' he apologised to Adele with a crooked smile. 'I wondered if you'd do me a favour.'

Adele, reclining on the damask sofa, the light from the green-gold table lamp bathing her in its glow, set aside her magazine at the sight of the tawny-haired girl in the doorway. There was no doubt that she had recognised Stephanie from the photographs she had seen in the paper alongside Neal's, in the days when the smuggling scandal had been in the news. Quick to make it known, she drawled, 'Why, of course, Neal. This is your stewardess friend, isn't it?'

'That's right—Stephanie Keynes. Steve, this is Mrs Adele Downing. Steve's come for a stay on New Providence, but since I'm a bachelor it wouldn't be right to guest her at my house. I wondered if you'd mind putting her up here at Medway?'

With a flicker of impatience mingling with smiling tolerance Stephanie stepped forward. 'I've already explained to Neal that I don't mind gossip. I mean, these days who cares what——'

'It's not just gossip,' Neal cut in. 'Family connections go deep on the island and there are certain standards of behaviour we like to uphold.'

While Stephanie changed her expression to one of suitable understanding Adele said with an intrigued look her way, 'She's welcome to stay here, Neal. There's a bed aired and made up in a room next to ours. I'm sure she'll be very comfortable.'

'Thanks, Adele. I knew I could count on you.' He went out and returned a moment later with Stephanie's bags. 'Well, that's that fixed up.' As he straightened, his gaze wandered to where Laraine was curled up in her chair. Looking decidedly masculine amidst the scene of feminine domesticity, he said briefly, 'You two have met, I believe? 'Stephanie smiled largely across the room and it occurred to Laraine that Neal might be taking convention a little too far. After all, he did retain umpteen servants and their families at his house, so he could hardly be considered to be living alone. 'Goodnight, Steve,' she heard him saying. 'I'll be along to pick you up in the morning. Sleep well.' She watched Stephanie go out with him to the car and sank deeper into her chair, swallowed up by black despair and unbearable unhappiness.

Adele rang for Benjamin and as he prepared to show Stephanie to her room she was told, 'Do make yourself entirely at home, and when you've changed into something more comfortable come down and join us, won't you?'

'Thank you, I'd like to.' Stephanie replied with such smiling alacrity, one sensed at once the common bond that some women have with each other. She reappeared a short while later in a smart housecoat, her hair tumbling over its tailored shoulders, and Adele invited, 'Help yourself to a drink. The cabinet's over there.'

'That's very kind of you, Mrs Downing.'

'Call me Adele.' She watched with irony as the guest poured out spirit liberally and came away with a glass three-quarters full.

Stephanie went to the other armchair and dropped down, needing no more encouragement, it seemed, to make herself at home. She took a drink and said with a deep sigh of satisfaction, smiling at her glass, 'It's good to be back with Neal again. I've travelled halfway across the world to be with him, but it was worth it.'

'I take it the two of you are very close?' Adele queried.

'Very!' Stephanie replied, making the word sound loaded with meaning.

'In spite of the smuggling scandal?' Adele asked coyly. As this was a woman-to woman chat she clearly saw no reason to pretend that she was ignorant of the facts.

'It was upsetting for Neal,' Stephanie put on a look of fleeting compassion, then settled more comfortably, 'but I intend to make him forget all he's been through.'

Adele studied the other woman. After a moment she said something which made Laraine warm to her.

'I know Neal very well.' Adele was fingering the pages of her magazine. 'He doesn't strike me as a man who would flaunt the law in forbidden transactions.'

'No, unfortunately he was the innocent party,' Stephanie almost drained her glass of its contents. 'He didn't say anything at the hearing to protect me.'

She was smiling, so Adele smiled too as woman to woman, then she asked after some time had elapsed, 'Just what did happen to create all the fuss within the airline company?'

Stephanie shrugged, already on intimate terms with her hostess. 'We were moving some stuff—I won't say what—from France. Frank Tate, he's a steward friend of mine, was supposed to be on the receiving end, but something went wrong, and Neal being the captain of the flight was held responsible for the . . . contraband goods aboard.'

'So Neal could have just put the finger on you both and that would have been the end of it,' Adele mused aloud.

'Yes, but Neal's not like that,' Stephanie looked both contrite and content. 'The unfavourable publicity would have been unbearable for me, and both Frank and I would have lost our jobs.'

'Instead Neal had his career ruined,' Adele murmured.

'I suppose so,' Stephanie considered vaguely, 'but as I say, I intend to make it up to him. Neal loved me long before the trouble blew up. I still feel the same way about him, and as I've told him, what's gone need have no further effect on our lives.'

Feeling slightly sick, Laraine put down the book she had been ostensibly reading and, rising, she said, 'It's getting late. If you two don't mind, I think I'll go to bed.'

As she went out the pair moved on to other topics of

intimate conversation and as she climbed the stairs Laraine wondered, was a woman who had done what Stephanie had done to Neal capable of love?

CHAPTER THIRTEEN

LARAINE rummaged through her things wondering slackly what she could wear for Conrad's visit. His ship had docked and he had rung up ten minutes ago and excitedly told her he was on his way over.

In the past few days she had given a lot of thought to Conrad. Never realising before how close they had become through his constant dropping in at Medway, she supposed the idea of their making a permanent match was not something to be discarded lightly. She couldn't go on living with Adele, that would be impossible, and forlornly she recalled Stephanie's glowing features each evening when she returned from a day spent with Neal. Conrad was a sweet person, but there was a serious side to him. He would probably go far in the world, get to be an Admiral like his father and his grandfather before him. Though this thought didn't excite Laraine very much, she knew that she would be safe and secure with Conrad. Yes, she glumly held up a sun-dress of cotton print before her at the mirror, she would do whatever Neal decided for her.

They spent the afternoon in the grounds of Medway, wandering along rose-strewn paths and resting in blossom-shaded arbours. Conrad, boyishly handsome in his gold-braided uniform which he hadn't had time to change, was bursting with undisclosed designs, but he kept himself in check until the sun began to cast its reflection on the sea and he would soon have to return to Nassau.

Then he took Laraine nervously by the hand and told

her, 'I've got to pay a call on Neal. Do you know if he's free at the moment?'

'No, there's someone at the house just now,' Laraine explained, thinking of Stephanie with a weight round her heart.

'Pity.' Conrad's grin was uncertain. 'I've got to talk to him about us.'

'Yes, he told me,' said Laraine with a view to easing the situation.

Conrad looked at her with a leaping expression. 'Then you know how I feel about you?'

'I think I do,' she smiled.

'Oh, Laraine!' He took her into his arms. 'I never thought it would be so difficult to get it out. Will you have me? Will you put up with a sailor's life just to put this poor mutt out of his misery? I promise you, you'll never be neglected. I'll put in for a shore job first.'

Striving not to douse his enthusiasm, Laraine replied, 'I like you, Con. I like you a lot.'

His laughing eyes viewed her questioningly. 'Am I going to have to be satisfied with that?' He kissed her then, and there was nothing she could do but return his affection in a way that would not diminish his happiness.

A long time later, after releasing her, he cursed under his breath. 'I've got to spend my leave with Timothy Marshways over at Culberts Bay—friends of the family, unfortunately, so there's no ducking the invitation. They're sending a car to the ship for me at six-thirty.' He looked at his watch. 'Oh hell, it's almost that now. But when we've talked to Neal,' he grabbed her hand as they hurried, 'you'll be able to pack your bags and come over to the Marshways' with me. I've no doubt they'll put on a big spread for our engagement party. My parents might even fly out from England to meet you.'

He bundled into his decrepit car and waved madly in the horrendous din as it took off. Laraine waved vigorously in return in the hope of dispelling any uncertainty that Conrad might be experiencing.

As she returned to the house she thought of Stuart's interest in charting blue holes, and Conrad's much more important Naval job of charting territorial waters. Two men with similar goals but contrasting personalities, who, in their way, were very dear to her.

The following day Adele told her that she had decided to spend a few days at the Coral Reef Country Club. Laraine was uneasy at the news but not really surprised. Stuart didn't come to Medway, but his boat was anchored at the Country Club harbour. Putting up in one of the luxurious suites, Adele would be on hand to angle for any lazy invitations that might be going to sail with Stuart on his yawl.

Adele packed her own bag and, making it abundantly clear that this was one time when Laraine wasn't needed, eagerly accepted a lift from a tree doctor who had come from Nassau to do his periodic check of the grounds of Medway. Laraine watched her go, pondering sadly on the ironies of fate. Adele, who had never given her heart to any man in her life was now holding it cupped in outstretched hands. And there was no one there to receive it, least of all Stuart, who was content to live in the past with his memories of June Shor. What a pity she couldn't have felt like that about Richard. Laraine blinked back the tears. But life wasn't like that.

She turned indoors, supposing that she might as well start packing her own things. Conrad would be phoning Neal any time and she might as well be ready to move out when the time came. She would have to call in at the Club, of course, and tell Adele that she was going to marry Conrad, but from what she had seen of her sister-in-law lately she guessed she would take the news indifferently.

Laraine wondered at herself and at her calm acceptance of the inevitable. She didn't love Conrad, she loved Neal, but Neal had told her she should marry Conrad, and loving him she was prepared to do as he wished, bleak though the prospect was of saying goodbye to Neal for ever. But he would never notice her going, not now that Stephanie had come back into his life.

She worked for a while in her room, but it was hard to feel any zest for what she was doing and the outdoors beckoned if only as a soothing influence on her aching heart. There was something easing, be it fractionally, in wandering under a blue sky with nature colouring one's views. It hurt her to wonder what Woodes was thinking about her desertion, but the beach was as near as she would let herself go with Stephanie spending all her time next door.

She was scuffing through the sand idly looking for shells when Neal appeared. How her heart would have leapt if it had been like the old times, but he was looking about him slightly askance, and she knew he was on the beach because there was something wrong.

He approached, and his stricken expression tugged at something that lay buried beneath the weight of Laraine's unhappiness. Apprehension stirred in her.

'Woodes has gone,' His words drained the last vestige of courage from her. 'He got through a gap in the fence, I think, and he hasn't been back all night. I've searched the grounds and the fields. I thought he might have been down here on the beach, but it seems there's no luck.'

'Oh Neal!' Laraine's eyes brimmed. Glistening there were tears for Woodes, but tears too because Stephanie had come back and her whole world had fallen apart.

'He's a tramp at heart, Laraine,' Neal said gently. 'You've got to accept that.'

'I suppose you're right,' she nodded, trying to brighten. 'But he's not forced to have taken to his old ways. He might be trotting around somewhere quite close to here. I'm sure he could be.'

'I doubt it.' Neal shook his head. 'I've combed every

inch of the area. Woodes is a city dog. It's my bet he's gone to join his alley pals in Nassau.'

'And leave all this?' Laraine cast a glance at the country views. 'I won't believe that.'

Neal seemed aware of the passing of time. 'I've got to be getting back to Stephanie,' he said. 'Will you be okay?'

'Yes, I'm all right,' Laraine smiled through her sniffles. She couldn't let Neal see how miserable she was.

He left her on the beach and when he was out of sight she began her own search for Woodes. She would find him. She was sure she would find him.

The cars that went by on the road were few and far between, but when they came they hurtled past like speeding monsters and Laraine had to stand well into the side to miss the gust of tires. In the two days that Woodes had been missing she had little hope now of coming across him, but still she couldn't stop the search. It was as though by punishing her body with this endless routing over the countryside she would deaden the feeling of desolation that engulfed her.

She peered into a ditch at the side of the road, ever hopeful of seeing a powder-puff shape sniffing there, then had to move on again at the sound of another vehicle. As it approached she recognised it as Neal's car. Stephanie was seated beside him, neat and attractive as always. Laraine's heart sank when he pulled in beside her. She would have preferred them to have given just a wave in passing, then she could have pretended that the sight of them together affected her in no way at all.

But Neal was not in a waving mood. He viewed her grimly and said, 'Jordan told me he saw you mooning about on the road yesterday. You've got to forget Woodes, Laraine. Get it into your head that he's gone, left the area.'

Forget Woodes! Laraine confronted him with a flash of tears. 'I don't intend to wash my hands of him just like that,' she said hotly. She didn't care what she looked like in her old frayed shorts and knotted beach-top. She had long since lost interest in putting on sophisticated airs.

'And what good do you think you're doing risking your neck on a main highway?' Neal snapped. 'I don't want to hear any more tales about you wandering alone out here, understand?'

She tried not to appear meek, but she had no fight left in her where Neal was concerned. His gaze told her that he was touched by her forlorn appearance, and she would have given anything to be able to look robust and worldly uncaring, but what could she do, loving him as she did?

He let the breath ease out tolerantly from between his teeth, then opened the door. 'Get in. I'll take you back to Medway.'

At this Stephanie's face crumpled in a look of displeasure. She had been viewing the situation with detached amusement, but now she complained, 'But Neal, that's in the opposite direction to where we're going! And it's quite a drive to Adelaide beach. Do we have to waste our time with nursery chores?'

'I'm not leaving Laraine to walk back along this lonely stretch,' said Neal, getting out to make sure that she obeyed his demands and slamming the door shut tight after her. 'You'll just have to put up with the delay.'

The drive back to Medway was made in silence. Neal left the car to escort Laraine along the drive and in the doorway he said, gently now, his hand still on her arm 'Stop eating your heart out for the dog, little one. He'll be safe somewhere.'

About to leave, he turned back to say, 'Oh by the way, Jordan also tells me that Conrad's been trying to phone me all week.' His mouth was wry and they both knew there was no need to put into words that his time was fully occupied in escorting Stephanie around. He added, 'He's coming over on Saturday evening. You'd better be at my house too. About seven.'

'Yes, Neal,' Laraine nodded.

'And chin up, remember!' He gave her an encouraging grin. She made an effort to smile and with a lingering look, his grin tightening at the corners, he left her.

Stephanie had never much to say to Laraine and it didn't please her when she was compelled to stay at Medway for lunch the next day. Neal had been in Nassau all morning and he actually didn't turn up to take her out until after three. However, Stephanie was a past master at masking her annoyance and she greeted him with a pleasant smile.

Neal looked a littly weary, but he had obviously made plans. 'I've got the Cherokee all set for that flip you wanted to take over the bay,' he told her. He was leading the way out when his glance came to rest, not for the first time since his arrival on Laraine, preparing to drift off to the beach. 'You can come too, kitten,' he said, beckoning.' The change will do you good.'

Stephanie's annoyance surfaced at this and for once she didn't bother to hide it. 'But Neal! I thought it was going to be just the two of us,' she railed harshly.

But Neal's mouth was set. 'The child's upset. Can't you see that?' he snapped. And then in easier tones, 'Don't worry, she can sit in the back.'

Mollified, Stephanie had no choice but to agree. Laraine had little choice either, with Neal's hand on her arm, though she could think of nothing more trying in her present state of abject unhappiness than a session in the company of Stephanie and Neal. A few minutes later when they boarded the Cherokee on the strip adjoining Neal's house she moved thankfully to one of the seats at the rear.

Stephanie made all the right exclamations as they flew over the coral-hued depths out at sea. Laraine viewed the sparkling waves dully. Out of kindness Neal had brought her up here to take her mind off the missing Woodes. She didn't know then that all else was about to be wiped from her mind in a terrifying brush with the unexpected, the outcome of which was to prove a matter of life and death.

They had been flying about twenty minutes when the call signal sounded in the little cabin. Neal answered the flashing light, introduced himself, then they were all surprised to hear Adele's voice on the line. 'Neal! Thank God I've managed to contact you!' She sounded strained and on edge. 'Something awful's happened. It's Stuart——' She broke down and there was a horrible silence before she remembered to switch over so that Neal could talk.

He spoke coolly. 'Pull yourself together, Adele, and listen. I'm going to ask the questions and I want you to answer as precisely as possible, is that clear? Now first of all, what's the trouble? Over.'

Adele explained, but not very coherently. 'He found an underwater cavern—Stuart—he wanted to go down to investigate—he was going to come back to the boat for some photographic equipment, but he hasn't surfaced—Oh, Neal, I'm so worried! In a few minutes he'll have no more oxygen supply.'

'How many times have I told that son of a clown not to go down on his own?' Neal allowed himself a curse under his breath, then spoke levelly again. 'Who's with you on the yawl, Adele? And are there any other vessels in the vicinity?'

'Jimbey's here and Waldo—it was him who told me how to work this radio thing—no one else around—no boats——'

Laraine's heart sank at this news. Jimbey and Waldo were the two native Bahamians who helped Stuart on the yawl, but they were both elderly and of little use, it seemed.

Neal was already preparing himself for action. 'Adele, can you tell me exactly where you are?'

'Oh, you can't expect me to know about charts and things.' She sounded exasperated. They all knew that time was running out. Distractedly she paused to think. 'We sailed out from Yamacraw beach not long ago, if that's any help.'

As Neal signed off his tones were encouraging. 'Don't worry, Adele, we'll find you.'

He banked away and a few seconds later at the whine and rumble of something happening to the undercarriage he spoke aloud. 'That's the sea-skids sliding into position. We'll be able to come down close to the *Melanie*.' He knew just where he was going and they spotted her almost at once in the vast expanse of blue-green ocean, a moth-like object which soon became a real live yawl, scene of the palpitating mishap, as they flew in low to land on the waves.

A skiff was sent over and Neal saw to it that they all transferred to the yawl in the shortest possible time. Adele looked white with worry. Waldo, stripped down to shorts and the more athletic of the two men, met Neal with a spate of words his eyes popping. 'I been down dere, mahn.' He pointed a dripping finger towards the deep. 'He stuck—got one arm and his oxygen pack jammed in a crevice. There was nothing I could do. I been down for sponges, but, mahn, I ain't got no breath now.'

The other man was looking dolefully into the dark depths. 'I remind the time when——'

'Save your memories.' Neal was already stripping. 'Get me some scuba gear quick, and a rock axe or something.'

Laraine tried to comfort her sister-in-law. 'Don't worry, Adele. Stuart's going to be all right, I'm sure he is.' She spoke with an optimism that she was far from feeling.

Neal was over the side within seconds of landing on the yawl, but the minutes that followed were the longest and most harrowing that Laraine had never known. At times she was stricken with the thought that Neal too would succumb in his battle to save Stuart, and as the long moments stretched she felt almost faint with panic and anxiety.

In the silence stretching to distant horizons it seemed that there could not possibly be life now below the waves, then the surface broke and Neal appeared, bearing a prostrate Stuart in his arms.

Adele gave a little scream when she saw him. He was greyfaced and his eyes were closed as though for ever. But Neal tried to sound heartening. 'He's alive, Adele, but he's got to have medical attention, and fast.'

As he relieved Stuart of his driving impedimenta and lowered him into the skiff to take him to the plane Adele rushed forward. 'I'm going with him. Do you hear? I'm going too——'

'Adele, don't upset yourself!' Laraine put out a soothing hand.

'Get in, the two of you,' Neal commanded. 'We've no time to lose.'

Stephanie stepped forward, her face pinched. 'And what about me?' she asked.

'Sorry, Steve, the girls are family.' Neal was already casting off.

'But you're not going to leave me here!' Stephanie was angrily incredulous.

'There's only room for four in the plane,' said Neal over his shoulder. 'The boys will take you back.'

They left Stephanie marching around indignantly and helplessly on deck.

In the Cherokee Adele cushioned Stuart's weight in the back and after drying off gratefully with the towel that Laraine had had the presence of mind to grab up Neal flew straight for the hospital in Nassau. There was another wait, several agonising hours before the blissful news came through that Stuart would live.

Stuart rapidly improved, but he had had a close brush with death and his convalescence was expected to be lengthy. As he was more or less a wheelchair case he had decided to return to England, and Neal and Laraine had seen him to say their goodbyes. He was pale and weak, but laconic as ever.

Back at Medway Laraine came upon Adele packing her things. 'I'm going with him, Larry,' she said without ceasing in her task. She was pale herself and only a shadow of the glamorous, seductive Adele of the past. 'I expect I'll be back one day to close up the house . . . I can't concern myself with business matters just now, but you'll cope for the moment, won't you, child?'

Laraine didn't say anything about her own plans. It was hardly the time to mention her engagement to Conrad. Adele embraced her. In that moment Laraine was stirred by a strange bond of affection between the two of them. Her sister-in-law had changed. Love had brought with it humility for others and understanding.

With Adele's going Medway wore a melancholy air which Stephanie's presence did little to allay. The latter said very little while she was compelled to stay at the house, which was often now, since Neal was spending a great deal of his time in Nassau. But he would be in this evening. Laraine stood before the mirror wondering what she could do about her lacklustre appearance. Today was Saturday and in a little while Conrad would be calling on him and asking, with true old-fashioned courtesy, for her hand in marriage.

Stephanie had taken Adele's hired car, as she was in the habit of doing now, and driven over to Neal's about an hour ago. Laraine disliked the idea of going while the two of them were together. But perhaps Neal wanted it like this. Maybe he was going to announce that there was to be a double wedding; his with Stephanie, as well as hers with Conrad.

Dispiritedly she made some effort to get ready. Later, in the dusky pink silk dress and a suitable pair of shoes, she considered she had done her best for Conrad. She could do nothing about her shadowed eyes, of course, and the haunting sadness there, but perhaps if she smiled a lot, no one would notice.

The stars were taking on a brilliance over the muted ocean as she went down the beach trail. Traversing the now well-worn path through Neal's meadow, it came to her that he had never complained about her ruining his ploughed land. She blinked back a brightness in her eyes at all that was lovingly familiar to her. After tonight she was going to have to stop thinking about Neal. Conrad would be her husband and he deserved something better than lukewarm affection.

The lights were on in the house, spilling out from the rear windows and casting a golden glow over the back garden area. Laraine received a small shock when she went in at the gate. On the path a nuzzling shape writhed about her ankles. It was a little black and white dog with soft ears and a bushy tail. Laraine patted her protruding ribs. She was a stray, obviously. She wondered absently if this one too had been caught stealing the day's joint, but the thought caused her no amusement. It reminded her too painfully of Woodes.

She decided to sit on a stone bench and wait. It was almost seven, so Neal would know she was out here somewhere. There was no need to go in until Conrad arrived. She hadn't realised how the voices carried through the open doorway of Neal's lounge until she had actually become seated. She thought of moving, but he spoke in such clear-cut tones that it was doubtful if she would have escaped them anywhere in the area.

There was the sound of glasses and liquor being poured. Then with a clink Neal said, 'This will be our last drink together, Stephanie.'

Her laugh was uncertain. 'I'm not sure I know what you mean by that, Neal.'

'I mean that I won't be seeing you again after tonight.'

As though the reply was not entirely unexpected the feminine tones became slightly venomous. 'So that's it!

This is what I get for coming all these thousands of miles to see you!'

'You've travelled a long way, but I could have told you at the beginning that your journey was fruitless,' said Neal.

Stephanie seemed to be contesting this with everything she could muster. 'You loved me.' Her voice came over thinly. 'I was the only woman in your life.'

'I used to think so. I know now I was wrong about us. Working in close contact with someone can give one false ideas.' Perhaps Neal shrugged his shoulders. 'I can assure you I shall feel no remorse at your departure.'

'You needn't think you're getting rid of me just like that!' The venom was more than noticeable now.

Neal said, 'I've taken the liberty of having your things packed and brought over. I can also tell you there's a plane going your way due out at eight-thirty, so you should make it quite comfortably. You can leave Adele's car at the airport. I'll pick it up later.'

The fuming opposition was made silently and Neal added, 'Go back to Frank, Stephanie. That's where you belong.'

'I will!' she spat. 'And don't think either of us will lift a finger to clear your name!'

'I wouldn't expect it of you,' Neal said suavely. 'Shall we go?'

Laraine listened to the departing footsteps. So Neal had joined the league of unbelievers, she thought sadly. It would have been almost better if he had married Stephanie rather than end up like Stuart.

A few seconds later she heard the angry screeching away of the car, bringing a curious lifting of the air with Stephanie's departure.

Neal came back through the house and out of the open lounge doorway. He appeared to take Laraine's presence on the bench as a matter of course. The little black and white dog came fussing round him. He said, patting her warmly, 'I found her chewing vegetable rubbish behind the house. She's been here a couple of days now. Getting used to the place, I think.'

'She's adorable,' Laraine smiled wanly.

Neal's green eyes had a peculiar merry light in them, 'Come on out front.' He took her hand. 'I've got something to show you.'

She went with him not knowing what to expect. At his car on the drive she thought she saw a movement in the glow of the interior. And then at her appearance the movement became a scrabbling, yapping shape and she cried, 'Woodes!'

He had been lying down obediently on a rug in the back, but now he was all set to hurl himself at her, which was precisely what he did when Neal opened the door. 'I wanted to keep him in the car as a surprise,' said Neal, watching her happiness with a tolerant grin. 'I found him down at the port hobnobbing with some of his dock pals. He's been shampooed and deloused yet again.'

'Oh, Woodes, you are a headache! But I do love you,' Laraine laughed through contented tears. She led him through the house on his lead and let him off at the back where he swaggered about, showing off to the other guest that he was an old hand at this domesticity lark. The little black and white dog fawned around him eager for affection and though he kept her at a respectable distance it was obvious he found this kind of hero-worship considerably pleasing.

'I don't think we need have any more worries about Woodes,' Neal said succinctly. 'There's nothing like a woman for keeping man in his place.'

She met the laughter in Neal's eyes, then, her joy short-lived, she asked, looking at her watch, 'I wonder where Conrad is?'

'He left some time back.' At her astonished glance Neal added, 'He came early at my request.' He led her to where the sea was visible under the stars and went on, 'I gave him my answer, and he didn't take it too badly. He's a career man, is young Conrad. I think he knows that a wife just now might hamper his promotion.'

'But I don't understand.' Laraine's mind was in a whirl. Had Conrad guessed after all that she didn't feel that way for him? She spoke aloud. 'What was it you said to him?'

'I told him that I was going to marry you myself. He didn't seem all that surprised.' As he drew her into his arms Neal's teasing gaze was suddenly serious. 'I am right, aren't I? I'm not just seeing things that——'

'Oh, Neal!' Laraine couldn't believe that she was being gripped fiercely close by him. But when his lips found hers there was no doubt in her mind that what she had lovingly imagined was really happening.

After the heady wonder of his kiss, during which she left him in no doubt either, he viewed her with an agonised look in his eyes. 'And to think I almost drove you into McKelway's arms.'

'Was I that much of a threat to your independent male existence?' she gleamed saucily.

He ran a hand through her hair and became smilingly introspective. 'You've been on my mind for a long time, but I kept remembering Stephanie and I considered I'd had enough romantic attachments to last me a lifetime. When you went away with Stuart I could have cheerfully strangled him—that's how bad it got with me.' He gave her a rueful grin. 'It was okay when I could regard you as a kid in the background, but then you started getting womanly ways, and a man has no protection against your kind of feminine charms.'

Laraine's heart was singing to know that this man hadn't. But there was something else she wanted to hear.

'Was there never anything between you and Adele?' she asked.

'Nothing,' Neal shook his head. 'I found her company just right for putting the cheating ways of Stephanie out of my mind. She was always there to remind me what a fool I'd been to have trusted another such smooth woman as herself.'

'She's desperately in love with Stuart,' said Laraine.

'I know. I've seen it coming for a long time.'

At Neal's heavy reply she asked, 'Do you think that one day they may get together?'

'It's difficult to say. Stuart's pretty set in his ways. And then there's June Shor.'

'I know,' Laraine nodded pensively. Poor Adele! Poor Stuart.

Neal gripped her close as though aware more than ever of what he had almost lost. She broke the silence to mention, 'I heard what you said to Stephanie.'

'I wanted you to,' Neal said a little grimly. 'I planned it that way. When Stephanie first arrived it was my intention to show her a little of New Providence—she'd come a long way—and then tell her that there was little point in her staying on. But then Woodes' disappearance blew up and she got rather neglected, I'm afraid, while I was scouting Nassau for him. That precipitated the whole thing, so there was little explaining to be done. She more or less got the message, I think.'

'But you're still carrying the blame for the smuggling scandal,' Laraine said worriedly.

'I don't think I will be for long.' Neal looked grimly amused. 'Frank Tate is in trouble again, I hear, and there's likely to be another inquiry. It's all bound to come out this time, so it's more or less certain I'll be put in the clear.'

'Will you go back to the airline company?' Laraine asked with a sudden lurch of her heart.

'No, I've found contentment here in this old family house and the land is now my life—if you're willing to share it with me, my darling.'

'Oh, Neal!' She clung to him as he held her close. 'Nothing would make me happier.' Woodes at that moment tried to get in on the act and sparing a hand to fondle him she said with shining-eyed wonder, 'You spent all that time, all those days hunting around Nassau, just for me!'

'I couldn't bear to see your unhappiness.' Neal kissed her ear-lobe tenderly. 'It also let me see that in the future we were going to be two very unhappy people, so I decided to forget my plans to stay aloof from romance and trade it all in for the love of my life.' His lips were suddenly demanding and against her mouth he asked, 'Tell me . . . none of it was my imagination, that night on Little Farmers' Cay, was it?'

'None of it,' she confessed, quivering at his nearness.

'We'll go there again for our honeymoon,' he said gruffly. 'Let's make it soon, my love . . . after all, we owe it to old Adam. . . .'

'Oh?' She turned him to meet her twinkling gaze, having a fair idea of what was coming. 'And why do we owe it to Adam?'

'Well, we both know he's itching to see his first grandchild.' Neal looked wickedly innocent. While she was colouring prettily, he added impulsively, 'I know what we'll do! We'll go to town right now and tell him. That should put his mind at rest. And then we'll go to dinner at the Bridge Inn on East Bay Street and afterwards drive alongside the beach by moonlight. How does that sound?'

'Heavenly!' Laraine sighed with his lips in the hollow of her throat. But she was thinking of another heaven; where the moonlight silvered a crescent of white sand and its encircling palms. She had called it Dream Island, and she knew now that dreams came true!

Harlequin Plus

A GREAT EXPLORER

It is taught that Christopher Columbus "discovered" America, but there is no evidence that he ever landed on the North American mainland. His journeys took him to the Caribbean Islands and farther south.

Born in Genoa, Italy, in 1451, Cristoforo Colombo was a sea-loving, adventurous youth who dreamed of discovering a new world. It was the golden era of European exploration, and Columbus wanted to be the first navigator to reach Asia by sailing west, thus proving that the earth was round. For eight years he tried to get support for his expedition, and finally he was sponsored by King Ferdinand of Spain.

In 1492 he set sail from Spain with a fleet of three ships. Two months later, he became the first European to land in what is known today as the Bahamas, where he claimed the first island he saw for Spain.

For ten years Columbus sailed freely between Europe and the Caribbean; he discovered Cuba, Hispaniola, Jamaica and most of the Caribbean islands, as well as the northern coast of South America. Mistakenly believing that he had reached India, he called the natives "Indians" and subjected them to rigid rule. It wasn't long before uprisings broke out—particularly in Hispaniola; Columbus was held responsible by a Spanish royal commission and was sent back to Spain in chains and stripped of his political powers. He was permitted one more expedition, but when he returned for the last time to Spain, it was as a disillusioned man. The bold explorer whose hopes had once been so bright died in poverty and neglect.

FREE!
Romance Treasury

A beautifully bound, value-packed, three-in-one volume of romance!